CU00835755

# The
# Flopperty Bird
## and
## Other Stories
by
ENID BLYTON

*Illustrated by*
Lesley Smith

AWARD PUBLICATIONS LIMITED

For further information on Enid Blyton please contact
www.blyton.com

ISBN 1-84135-433-3

This edition entitled *The Flopperty Bird and Other Stories*
published by permission of Enid Blyton Limited

First published by Award Publications Limited 2002
This edition first published 2005

Published by Award Publications Limited, The Old Riding
School, Welbeck Estate, Nr Worksop, Notts S80 3LR

Printed in Singapore

# CONTENTS

# The Flopperty Bird

The flopperty bird belonged to Winky the gnome. It was a big bird, with lovely long tail-feathers. Winky was very proud of it, and looked after it well. One day the flopperty bird said, "You are good to me, Winky. You may pull one of my tail-feathers out, and make a wish with it!"

Winky was excited. He pulled a feather out, and called his friend Longshanks the giant over to help make a wish.

"What will you wish for?" asked the giant.

"Something you can share with me," said Winky, "because you gave me the flopperty bird when it was a chick."

They decided to wish for something they were both very fond of. "I wish for a big raspberry tart!" said Winky.

There was a thud behind them, and an enormous tart, steaming hot and smelling delicious, appeared. They set to work, and soon finished it.

"Thank you for sharing it, Winky," said the giant. "Now I must go home, or my wife will be cross."

He was late for dinner, and his wife, who was a witch, was very cross indeed. "Sit down and eat your dinner at once!" she snapped.

"Oh dear, I don't want any," said the giant. "I'm not hungry!"

"What have you been eating?" asked his wife. The giant told her.

"What!" she cried. "You wasted a wish on a raspberry tart!"

"A fine wish it was too!" said the giant. "In fact, I'd like another one!"

"You might have had gold, or a palace, or a kingdom!" stormed the witch.

The giant said nothing more, but the witch thought and thought.

"If the flopperty bird has any more wish feathers, it's no good silly Winky or stupid big Longshanks having them," she decided. "I shall have them!"

So that night she took a big pair of scissors, crept into Winky's cottage, and with one snip cut off all the other tail-feathers of the poor flopperty bird. He woke up and began to squawk, while the witch rushed away into the darkness.

When she got home she went down to the cellar. She had eight feathers, which she flung one by one into the air, each time saying, "I wish for a bag of gold!"

7

Immediately eight large sacks of gold appeared. Crowing and chuckling, the witch went to bed.

Winky and Longshanks were terribly upset about the flopperty bird's tail-feathers, but as hard as they searched, they couldn't find out who had taken them. Then one day Longshanks began to wonder why his wife kept disappearing so often.

He followed her quietly the next time she went down to the cellar. And there he stared in amazement at the sacks of gold, for he guessed it was his wife who had taken the flopperty bird's feathers. He ran to tell Winky and the bird.

"Take me to her!" said the bird. They surprised the witch, who was still in the cellar.

"I don't care!" she said, laughing, "I've got my sacks of gold!"

"You haven't!" cried the flopperty bird, and he laughed loudly.

"See!" said the witch, and shook a sack open. Out poured a stream of yellow grain! The magic had gone from the gold!

8

"Aha!" said the bird. "I think, as you have such nice corn, Mistress Witch, I'll stay a few weeks with you and feed on it, for then my tail will grow again!"

So he did, and each time the witch fed him, the flopperty bird gave her a good peck, just to teach her that greediness never did anyone any good!

# The
# Gossamer Elf

Everybody knew the Gossamer Elf. She was the cleverest dressmaker in the whole of Fairyland. You should have seen the dresses and cloaks she made!

"I think her autumn clothes are the best," said Twinks. "She made me a lovely dress last October out of a red creeper leaf. I went to lots of parties in it."

"She made me a cloak out of a pair of beech leaves," said Feefo. "It was a golden cloak, the prettiest I ever had."

"Her stitches are the finest I ever saw," said Tiptoe. "Well – they're so fine I can't see them! I used to think that the Gossamer Elf didn't sew our dresses at all, but just made them by magic. She doesn't, though; I've seen her sewing away with a tiny, tiny needle."

"Ah, but have you seen her thread?" said Twinks. "It's so fine and so strong that once she's put a stitch into a dress it never comes undone."

"What does she use?" said Feefo. "I'd like to get some. I'll go and ask her."

So she went to call on the Gossamer Elf. But the elf was out. She had left her door open and Feefo went inside. On a shelf she saw reels upon reels – but they were all empty. Not one reel had any thread on it. How strange!

Soon the Gossamer Elf came in. Feefo ran to her.

"I've come to ask you something. Where do you get your fine thread? I can't see any on your reels."

The Gossamer Elf smiled. "No – my reels are all empty now," she said. "But soon they will be filled again with the finest, silkiest thread. I always get my thread at this time of year, you know."

"Where from?" asked Feefo. "Can I get some too? Do let me. Take me with you and I'll buy some."

"I don't buy it," said the Elf. "Yes, you can come with me if you like. I'm starting out tomorrow morning at dawn. You can carry some of my empty reels with you. That will be a help."

So Feefo and the Gossamer Elf set out at dawn. They went to the fields. It was a lovely morning, and the sun shone softly from a blue sky.

"It's gossamer time now," said the elf. "Did you know that? Soon the air will be full of fine silken threads that will stretch across the fields everywhere. See

12

– you can spy some already, gleaming in the sun."

Feefo looked. Yes – she could see some fine, long threads stretching from the hedge above high up into the air. Soon there would be plenty of them.

"But what are those silky threads?" said Feefo in wonder. "Where do they come from? And who makes them?"

They climbed up the hedge together, using the prickles on the wild rose stems as steps. They soon got high up in the hedge. Then Feefo saw around her many tiny spiders – young ones, not much more than babies.

Some stood on leaves, some clung to stems, and all of them were doing the same thing. They were sending out long silken threads from underneath their bodies.

"They have their silk spinnerets there," said the elf. "Big spiders have too. They take the thread from their spinnerets. Watch that tiny spider. See the long thread coming out and waving in the air?"

"Oh, yes," said Feefo in surprise. She saw dozens of tiny spiders all doing the same thing. "But why are they all doing this, Elf? It seems very strange to me. They are not spinning webs."

"No, they are going out into the world to seek their fortunes," said the elf. "Each baby spider wants to leave the place where he was born. He wants to journey far away and find his own place to live. So he is sending out a long, long thread into the air – and then, when he has a long enough line, he will let the wind take him off into the air with his gossamer thread – and, like a tiny

14

parachutist, he will soar over the world, and then drop gently to ground."

"Goodness me!" said Feefo, astonished. "Look, there goes one, Elf. Away he goes on the wind."

The tiny spider had let go his hold of the leaf, and now, swinging gently on the end of his gossamer thread, he let himself be carried away on the breeze, exactly like a tiny parachutist. Feefo and the elf watched him soaring away, until he could no longer be seen.

"They're all doing it, all the baby spiders!" cried Feefo in delight. "Oh, look at them swinging away on their threads. The wind blows the threads away and the spiders go with them!"

They watched the curious sight for a little while. Then Feefo turned to the elf. "But, Elf," she said, "surely you don't take their threads away from the tiny spiders? That would be a most unkind thing to do."

"Of course I don't," said the elf. "How could you think I'd do that? No – once the spiders have made their journey and landed safely somewhere, they don't want their threads any more. So I collect them on my reels, you see. I wind them up carefully, and soon have all my reels full for my year's work."

"Well, what a good idea," cried Feefo. "Look – here comes a spider from far away; see him swinging down on the end of his line? Here he is, just beside us. Little spider, what an adventure you've had!"

"May I take your thread please, if you

don't want it any more?" asked the Gossamer Elf politely. "Oh, thank you. What a nice long one!"

She began to wind the gossamer round and round her reel. Soon the reel was full. The spider ran off to find himself a nice new home under a leaf. Maybe he would catch plenty of flies there, he thought. Soon he would spin a web, and wait for his dinner to come along and fly into it.

Another spider landed a little farther down. Feefo ran to him. As soon as he had cast off his gossamer she began to wind it round and round the reel she

carried. "What fun this is!" she thought. "Now I know why the Gossamer Elf has her name. How clever she is to think of this idea!"

Day after day, early in the morning, Feefo and the Gossamer Elf went out together and waited for the tiny spiders to land near them on their gossamer lines. Soon they had dozens and dozens of reels full of the fine silken thread.

"There. We've got enough!" said the elf at last. "Now I shall wait for the leaves to change colour, and soon I shall be hard at work again making winter dresses and cloaks and sewing them with the gossamer thread given me by the tiny spiders. I shall be very busy indeed this winter!"

So she is. She is making coats of blackberry leaves, crimson, yellow and pink; dresses of golden hazel leaves, trimmed with berries, and cloaks of brilliant cherry leaves. You should see them! But you can't see her stitches – they are made of the gossamer from the spiders.

Have you ever seen it? You really must. You can take some too, if you want, for the spiders won't need it again.

# The
# Poor Old Teddy

There was once a poor old teddy bear who belonged to a little girl called Jean. She didn't treat him very well, for she had pulled out an eye, and made one of his arms loose. She often left him out in the rain, so he looked very dirty, and always had a cold.

The other toys thought him a dirty, sniffy old creature, and they wouldn't let him live in the toy-cupboard with them.

"No, get away, Teddy," said the big doll, pushing him out. "We shall catch your cold."

So the teddy sat meekly by the window alone and wished he had a handkerchief. The baby doll had one in her pocket, but he knew she wouldn't lend it to him.

Now one autumn day Jean took her toys out into the garden and sat them on the seat. She played school with them, and pretended that the teddy was very naughty indeed.

"You are the only toy that is not listening to your lessons!" she said to him. "You are very naughty. Go into the corner."

So the teddy had to sit down and turn his face to the bushes in the corner. He didn't really mind much, because, you see, he knew it was pretending. But what he did mind a great deal was being forgotten afterwards!

When the time came for Jean to take in her toys she forgot all about the teddy. She gathered up the toys on the seat, and took them indoors into the warmth and brightness of the house. But poor old Teddy was left standing out there in the dark and cold. He was very lonely and miserable.

He stood there until he was almost frozen. The frost came and pinched his toes. He shivered and shook, and began to sneeze. "A-tishoo! A-tishoo!"

Nobody was about. Nobody heard him. He shook himself and walked about to keep warm. It was very dark, and as he only had one eye to see with, he kept bumping into things. So altogether he was very miserable. He did wish he could meet a kind-hearted fairy, but as Jean didn't believe in fairies, there were none in her garden at all.

Teddy wandered about, and at last bumped into something hard and wooden. It was the dog's kennel! Sandy was inside, keeping himself warm in his bed. He woke up when he heard Teddy

bumping into his kennel, and growled.
Teddy trembled, and kept quite still.

Sandy ran out and sniffed around. He
found the teddy and smelled him all over.
He was puzzled.

"You're not a real animal," he said.
"Are you a toy? If you are, why aren't in
the playroom? Why are you wandering
about alone like this in the garden?"

"I am a toy," said the teddy. "I belong to Jean, but she left me out when she took the others in. I was so cold that I was walking about to get myself warm. I'm sorry I woke you up."

"Oh, so you belong to Jean, do you?" said Sandy. "Well, so do I, and I don't like it. Do you know, she sometimes forgets to give me fresh water in the morning? And look at my water now! Frozen hard! She won't notice in the morning that my water is frozen, and maybe I'll have nothing to drink tomorrow. Sometimes she forgets to give me biscuits, too, and often I don't get a run in the morning if she's playing with her toys, and doesn't want to bother to take me for a walk."

"A-tishoo!" said the bear. "I'm very sorry to hear what you . . . a-tishoo, a-tishoo – what you have to . . . a-tishoo! Do excuse me, I can't seem to stop sneezing, a-tishoo!"

"What a dreadful cold you have," said Sandy. "Come into my kennel and get warm."

"Oh, thank you so much," said the teddy gratefully. He crept into the kennel and snuggled down in the blanket. How warm it was! He cuddled up against Sandy. The dog liked it. It was nice to feel the teddy's little body snuggling into him.

"When I'm warm I'll fetch you some fresh water from the tap, if you like," said Teddy. "I know where the garden tap is, and I can just reach it."

"That's very good of you," said Sandy. "But don't bother tonight; I'm not at all thirsty."

Teddy fell asleep. He slept peacefully,

for he was warm and cosy. Sandy slept too. Neither of them woke until the morning. Then Teddy sat up, rubbed his one eye, and looked round in surprise. Wherever was he?

"Oh, of course, I'm in Sandy's kennel!" he said to himself. "And how much better my cold is! This warm kennel has almost sent it away."

"Hello, Teddy!" said Sandy. "So you are still there! I wondered if I had dreamed you."

"No, it was real," said Teddy. "Well, Sandy, thank you very much for letting me sleep with you. I suppose I'd better go back into the garden now and hope that Jean will remember me, and fetch me in."

"I don't see why you should go back to Jean at all," said Sandy. "Why not live with me here, in my kennel? There is plenty of room for both of us. I could keep you warm and play with you, and you could fetch me water or biscuits if Jean forgets them."

"Yes, and I could undo your chain and let you go for a run at night, if Jean doesn't take you out for a walk each day!" said the teddy, in excitement. "I could help you a lot, Sandy!"

"Well, let's do it then," said Sandy, giving the bear a lick on his nose. "I'd love to have you living with me. You're a nice little bear. Jean can't want you or love you if she leaves you out in the garden. She can just go without you!"

So the bear stayed in the kennel and didn't go out into the garden at all. Jean didn't remember him, so no one looked for him. When night came, the bear made his way out of the kennel, and said, "Sandy, Jean didn't give you fresh water, so I am going to get you some. You must be very thirsty. This has been frozen all day. You have had nothing to drink."

The teddy took a stone and cracked the ice in the drinking bowl. Then he emptied it all out and carried the bowl to the tap. It was heavy for him, but he managed it. He turned on the tap, and let some water run into the bowl. Then he turned off the tap and carried the bowl back carefully to the kennel. How glad Sandy was to have a good long drink! He had plenty of biscuits and a bone, for Jean had remembered those; but she hadn't taken him for a run, and he was longing to stretch his legs.

"I'll undo your chain now," said Teddy. He found it hard to undo at first, for he didn't know how to, but at last he managed it, and off went Sandy into the night, racing round and round the garden in delight. It was good to stretch

his legs when he had been still all day!

Sandy raced back to the kennel. "Get on my back, and I'll give you a ride," he said. So the teddy climbed up and held on tightly to Sandy's collar. Off they went, the bear grunting in delight. He had never in his life had such an exciting time before!

The two slept together peacefully. Teddy cuddled between Sandy's front paws and Sandy rested his head on the bear's chest. They were very good friends indeed.

Jean did look for Teddy, but she couldn't find him. She didn't think of looking in Sandy's kennel, of course! And anyway, Sandy said he would lie on top of Teddy and hide him if Jean did think of peeping in!

They still live together, and Teddy gives Sandy biscuits and water when Jean forgets, and lets him have a run every night. As for Teddy, he never has a cold now, and he is as happy as can be because somebody loves him and wants him.

I'd love to see him peeping out of Sandy's kennel, wouldn't you?

# The Little
# Singing Kettle

Curly the pixie lived all by himself in Twisty Cottage. His cottage stood at the end of the village of Ho, and was always very neatly kept. It had blue and yellow curtains at the windows and blue and yellow flowers in the garden, so you can guess how pretty and trim it was.

Curly was a mean pixie. He was the meanest pixie that ever lived, but he always pretended to be very generous indeed. If he had a bag of peppermints he never let anyone see it, but put it straight into his pocket till he got home. And if he met any of the other pixies he would pull a long face and say:

"If only I had a bag of sweets I would offer you one."

"Never mind," the other said. "It's

nice of you to think of it!" And off they went, saying what a nice, generous creature Curly was!

Now one day, as Curly was walking home along Dimity Lane, where the trees met overhead so that it was just like walking in a green tunnel, he saw a strange fellow in front of him. This was the Humpy Goblin, and he carried a great many saucepans, kettles and pans all slung down his back, round his shoulders and over his chest.

They made a great noise as he walked, but louder than the noise was the Humpy Goblin's voice. He sang all the time in a voice like a cracked bell:

"Do you want a saucepan,
    kettle or pan?
If you do, here's the goblin man!
The Humpy Goblin with his load
Of pots and pans is down the road,
Hie, hie, hie, here's the goblin man,
Do you want a saucepan,
    kettle or pan?"

Now Curly badly wanted a new kettle, because his own had a hole in it and the water leaked over his stove each day, making a funny hissing noise. So he ran after the goblin man and called him. The Humpy Goblin turned round and grinned. He was a cheerful fellow, always pleased to see anybody.

"I want a good little kettle, nice and cheap," said Curly.

"I've got just the one for you," said the Humpy Goblin, and he pointed to a

bright little kettle on his back. Curly
looked at it.

"How much is it?" he asked.

"Six silver pennies," said the goblin.
This was quite cheap, but mean old Curly
wasn't going to give six silver pennies
for the kettle. He pretended to be
shocked at the price, and then he gave a
huge sigh.

"Oh, I'm not rich enough to pay all
that," he said sadly. "I can only pay three
silver pennies."

"Oh, no," said the Humpy Goblin
firmly. "Three silver pennies isn't
enough. It costs six silver pennies."

Well, they stood and talked to one another for a long time, one saying six silver pennies and the other saying three silver pennies, until at last the Humpy Goblin laughed in Curly's face and walked off, jingling all his kettles and pans.

"You're a mean old stick!" he called after Curly. "I'm not going to sell you anything! Goodbye, Mr Mean!"

Off he went and soon began to sing his song again. Curly heard him.

"Do you want a saucepan,
    kettle or pan?
If you do, here's the goblin man!"

Curly stood and watched him angrily. Then he started walking too. He had to follow the goblin man because that was the way home to Twisty Cottage. But he took care not to follow too close, for he was afraid that the Humpy Goblin might call something rude after him.

It was a hot day and the goblin was tired. After a while he thought he would sit down in the hedge and rest. So down he sat – and it wasn't more than a minute before he was sound asleep and snoring! Curly heard him and knew he must be asleep. A naughty thought slipped into his head.

"I wonder if I could take that kettle from him while he's asleep? I could leave three silver pennies beside him to pay for it. How cross he would be when he woke up to find that I had got the kettle for three silver pennies after all!"

He crept up to the Humpy Goblin. He certainly was sound asleep, with his mouth so wide open that it was a good thing there wasn't anything above his head that could drop into it. Curly carefully undid the little shining kettle without making even a clink of noise. Then he put three bright pennies on the grass beside the goblin, and ran off, chuckling to himself for being so smart.

He soon reached home. He filled the little kettle with water and put it on the stove. It really was dear little thing, and it boiled very quickly indeed, sending a spurt of steam out of the spout almost before Curly had got out the teapot to make the tea.

Just as he had sat down to enjoy a cup of tea and a piece of cake, someone walked up his garden path and looked in at the door. It was the Humpy Goblin. When he saw that Curly had the kettle on the fire, he grinned all over his face.

"So you've got it!" he said. "Well, much good may it do you! Kettle, listen to me! Teach Mr Curly the lesson he needs! Ho, ho, Curly, you can keep the kettle! I don't want it!"

Laughing and skipping, the goblin went down the path again. Curly felt a bit uncomfortable. What was he laughing like that for?

"Oh, he just tried to frighten me and make me think something nasty would happen," said Curly to himself. "Silly old goblin!"

He cleared away his cup and saucer, and filled up the kettle again. He was washing up the dirty dishes when a knock came at his door, and Dame Pitapat looked in.

"I say, Curly, could you let me have a little tea? I've emptied my tin and it's such a long way to the shops."

Now Curly had a whole tin full, but he wasn't going to let Dame Pitapat have any. He ran to the dresser and took down a tin he knew was empty.

"Yes, certainly, Dame Pitapat," he said, "you shall have some of my tea. Oh, dear! The tin's empty! What a pity! You could have had half of it if only I'd had any, but I must have used it all up!"

Dame Pitapat looked at the empty tin. Then she turned to go.

"I'm sorry I bothered you, Curly," she said. "It was kind of you to say I could have had half, if only you'd had any tea."

Then a funny thing happened. The little kettle on the stove sent out a big spurt of steam and began to sing a shrill song:

> "Mister Curly has plenty of tea!
> He's just as mean as a pixie
>   can be!
> Look in the tin on the left
>   of the shelf
> And see what a lot he has
>   for himself!"

Then the kettle took another breath and shouted, "Mean old thing! Stingy old thing! Oooooh, look at him!"

Dame Pitapat was so astonished that she stood gaping for quite a minute. She couldn't think where the song came from. She had no idea it was the kettle on the stove. But Curly knew it was, and

41

he was so angry and ashamed that he could have cried.

Dame Pitapat went to the shelf and took down the tin that stood on the left. She opened it, and sure enough, it was full of tea to the brim.

"Oh, look at this!" she said. "Well, Curly, you said I could have half of any tea you had, so I shall take you at your word. Thanks very much."

She emptied half the tea out into the tin she had brought and went out of the cottage, looking round curiously to see if she could spy who had sung that song about Curly. But she didn't think of looking at the kettle, of course.

Curly was so angry with the kettle that he decided to beat it with a stick. But before he could do that someone poked his head in at the window and called him.

"Mr Curly! Will you lend me your umbrella, please? I've lost mine and it's raining."

It was little Capers, the pixie who lived next door. He was always lending Curly

things, and now he had come to borrow something himself. But Curly was in a very bad temper.

"My umbrella's lost too," he said. "I'm so sorry, Capers. You could have it if only I had it myself, but it's gone."

"Oh, well, never mind," said Capers. "It's nice of you to say you would have lent it to me."

Before he could go the shining kettle gave a tiny hop on the stove and began to sing again.

> "Mister Curly has got
>     an umbrella,
> He's such a mean and
>     stingy fella,
> He says he hasn't got one
>     at all
> But just you go and look in
>     the hall!"

Then it took another breath and began to shout again at the top of its steamy voice, "Mean old thing! Stingy old thing! Oooooh, look at him!"

Capers was so surprised to hear this song that he nearly fell in through the window. He stared at Curly, who was looking as black as thunder and as red as a beetroot. Then Capers looked through the kitchen door into the tiny hall – and sure enough Curly's green umbrella stood there.

Capers jumped in at the window and fetched the umbrella. He waved it at Curly.

"You said I could have it if only you had got it!" he cried. "Here it is, so I'll borrow it! Many thanks!"

He ran off and left Curly nearly crying with rage. The pixie caught up the stick and ran to beat the kettle – but that small kettle was far too quick for him! It rose up in the air and put itself high up on a shelf for safety. Then it poured just a drop of boiling water on to Curly's hand, which made the pixie dance and shout with pain.

"You wait till I get you!" cried Curly, shaking his stick.

Someone knocked at his front door. Curly opened it. Rag and Tag, the two gnomes, stood there smiling.

"Curly, we're collecting pennies for poor Mr Tumble whose house burned down yesterday," they said. "You are so generous that we thought you would be sure to give us one."

Curly knew that there was no money in his pockets, so he pulled them inside out quickly, saying, "Oh, yes, you shall have whatever money I have, Rag and

Tag. Goodness, there's none in this pocket – and none in that! How unfortunate! I haven't any pennies to give you, and I should have been so pleased to have let you have all I had."

"Well, that's very nice of you to say so," said Rag and Tag. "Never mind. Thank you very much for trying to be generous!"

Before they could go, that little kettle was singing again, spurting out great clouds of steam as it did so!

"Although he says he hasn't any,
Curly's got a silver penny!
Look in his purse on
     the table there
And take the money he well
     can spare!"

Then, taking another breath, the kettle shouted with all its might, "Mean old thing! Stingy old thing! Oooooh, look at him!"

Rag and Tag stared all round the kitchen to see where the voice came from, but they couldn't see anyone but Curly. It couldn't be the pixie singing, surely! No, he looked too angry and ashamed to sing anything!

The gnomes saw the purse lying on the table and they ran for it. Inside was a silver penny. They took it and put it into their box.

"Well, Curly," they said, "you said we

might have any pennies you had, if you'd had any – and you have, so we'll take this silver one. Goodbye!"

Out they went, giggling together, wondering who it was in the cottage that had given Curly away.

As for Curly, he was so angry that he caught up a jug of milk and flung it straight at the kettle, which was still high up on the shelf. *Crash!* The kettle hopped aside and the jug broke in a dozen pieces against the wall behind. The milk spilled and splashed all over Curly. Then the kettle began to laugh.

How it laughed! It was a funny, wheezy laugh, but you can't think how angry it made Curly!

He took up a hammer and flung that at the kettle too – but once more it slipped to one side, and oh dear me, a lovely big jar of plum jam up on the shelf was smashed. It all splashed down on to Curly, so what with milk and jam he was a fine sight. The kettle nearly killed itself with laughing. It almost fell off the shelf.

Curly went and washed himself under the tap. He felt frightened. What was he going to do with that awful singing kettle? He must get rid of it somehow or it would tell everyone the most dreadful tales about him.

"I'll wait till tonight," thought Curly. "Then, when it's asleep, I'll take it and throw it away."

So he took no more notice of the kettle, and as no other visitors came that day the kettle was fairly quiet – except that sometimes it would suddenly shout, "Mean old thing! Stingy old thing! Oooooooh, look at him!" Then Curly would almost jump out of his skin with fright, and glare at the kettle angrily.

At nine o'clock Curly went to bed. The kettle hopped down to the stove and went to sleep. Curly waited for a little while and then he crept out of bed. He went to the stove and took hold of the kettle. Ah, he had it now! The kettle woke up and shouted, but Curly had it by the handle. The water in it was no longer hot, so it could not hurt Curly.

The pixie hurried outside with the kettle and went to the bottom of his garden. There was a rubbish-heap there

and the pixie stuffed the struggling kettle
right into the middle. He left it there
and went back, delighted. He climbed
into bed and fell asleep.

But at midnight something woke him
by tapping at the window.

"Let me in!" cried a voice. "Let me in!
I'm dirty and I want washing!"

"That's that horrid kettle!" thought
Curly, in a fright. "Well, it can go on
tapping! I won't let it in!"

But the kettle tapped and tapped and at last it flung itself hard against the glass, broke it and came in through the hole! It went over to Curly's bed and stood itself there.

"Wash me!" it said. "I'm dirty and smelly. You shouldn't have put me on that nasty rubbish-heap!"

"Get off my nice clean bed!" cried Curly, angrily. "Look what a mess you are making!"

But the kettle wouldn't get off, and in the end the angry pixie had to get up and wash the kettle till it was clean again. Then he banged it down on the stove and left it.

Next day the kettle sang songs about him again, and Curly kept hearing it shout, "Mean old fellow! Stingy old fellow! Oooooooh, look at him!" till he was tired of it. So many people had heard about the strange things happening in the pixie's cottage that all day long visitors came to ask for different things, and poor Curly was nearly worried out of his life.

"I'll drown that kettle in my well tonight!" he thought. So once more he took the kettle when it was asleep and threw it down the well. *Splash!* Ha, it wouldn't get out of there in a hurry!

But about three o'clock in the morning there came a tap-tap-tap at the window, which had now been mended. It was the kettle back again!

"Curly! Let me in! I'm c-c-c-c-cold and w-wet! Let me in!"

Curly was afraid his window would be broken again, so he jumped out of bed and let in the shivering kettle. To his horror it crept into bed with him and wouldn't go away!

"It was cold and wet in the well!" said the kettle. "Warm me, Curly!"

So Curly had to warm the kettle, and how angry he was! It was so uncomfortable to sleep with a kettle, especially one that kept sticking its sharp spout into him. But he had to put up with it. In the morning he put the kettle back on the stove and started to think hard while he had his breakfast.

"I can't get rid of that kettle," he said to himself. "And while it's here it's sure to sing horrid things about me every time anyone comes to borrow something. I wonder what it would do if I let people have what they ask for? I'll try and see."

So when Mother Homey came and begged for a bit of soap because she had run out of it and the shops were closed that afternoon Curly gave her a whole new piece without making any excuse at all. Mother Homey was surprised and delighted.

"Thank you so much," she said. "You're a kind soul, Curly."

The kettle said nothing at all. Not a single word. As for Curly, he suddenly felt very nice inside. It was lovely to give somebody something. It made him feel warm and kind. He made up his mind to do it again to see if he felt nice the next time – and to see if that wretched kettle said anything.

He soon found that the kettle said never a word unless he was mean or untruthful – and he found, too, that it

was lovely to be kind and to give things away; it was nice even to lend them.

"I've been horrid and nasty," thought Curly to himself. "I'll turn over a new leaf and try to be different. And that old kettle can say what it likes! Anyway, it boils very quickly and makes a lovely pot of tea."

Very soon the kettle found little to say, for Curly became kind and generous. Once or twice he forgot, but as soon as he heard the kettle beginning to speak he quickly remembered, and the kettle stopped its song.

And one day who should peep in at the door but the Humpy Goblin, grinning all over his face as usual.

"Hello, Curly!" he said. "How did you like the kettle? Was it cheap for three silver pennies? I've come to take it back, if you want to get rid of it. It was a mean trick to play on you, really, but I think you deserved it!"

Curly looked at the smiling goblin. Then he took his purse from his pocket and found three silver pennies. He held them out to the Humpy Goblin.

"Here you are," he said. "You wanted six silver pennies for the kettle and I was mean enough to leave you only three. Here's the other three."

"But – but – don't you want to give me back the kettle?" asked the Humpy Goblin in surprise. "I left a horrid singing spell in it."

"Yes, I know," said Curly. "But I deserved it. I'm different now. I like the kettle too – we're great friends. I try to be kind now, so the kettle doesn't sing nasty things about me. It just hums nice, friendly little songs."

"Well, well, well, wonders will never end!" said the goblin man, astonished. "Don't bother about the other three silver pennies, Curly. I don't want them."

"Well, if you won't take them, let me offer you a cup of tea made from water boiled in the singing kettle," said Curly. The Humpy Goblin was even more astonished to hear the pixie being so kind, but he sat down at the table in delight.

Then he and Curly had a cup of tea

each and a large slice of ginger cake –
and they talked together and found that
they liked one another very much indeed.

So now Curly and the Humpy Goblin
are the very greatest friends, and the
little singing kettle hums its loudest
when it boils water for their tea. You
should just hear it!

# The
# Floating Duck

Once upon a time there was a lovely floating duck. She belonged to Janet, who floated her in the bath every night and loved her very much. When she was not in the bath she lived in the nursery toy-cupboard with the other toys.

One night the lead soldier began to quarrel with everyone. He often did this, because he was a bad-tempered little fellow. Also, he had a sword, and when he was in a very bad temper he liked nothing better than to draw his sword and prick people with it. It wasn't sharp enough to cut them, it could only prick them. It was very small and never did any damage, but how the toys did hate being chased by that tiny lead soldier waving his pin-like sword.

"Ooh! He's pricked me!" the curly-haired doll would cry, and she would slap him – but slaps never hurt him, for he was made of lead.

"Ooh! He's pricked me!" the teddy would cry, and he would kick the lead soldier over. But that didn't hurt him either.

One night he quarrelled with the floating duck. She happened to be beside him in the toy-cupboard.

"Move up!" he said to her. "You're squashing me!"

"I can't," said the duck. "The brick-box is on the other side of me."

"I shall prick you if you don't move," said the soldier, in his most quarrelsome voice.

"No, please don't," begged the duck. "If you make a hole in me I shan't be able to float."

"Run away from me then!" said the soldier. But the duck couldn't, for she had no legs. So the soldier pricked her with his sword and made a little hole in her body. Wasn't it dreadful?

Of course, when Janet floated her on
the bath that night, the poor duck filled
with water and sank to the bottom! Janet
was so upset. She took her out and said,
"Mummy! This duck won't float any
more! She's got a hole in her!"

When the duck got back to the nursery,
she wept and wept and wept. The toys
crowded round her and when they
discovered what had happened they were
so angry with the lead soldier that he
shivered in his boots and ran to hide in
the doll's-house.

Then the teddy had a good idea. He got a stick of sealing wax and melted a tiny drop of it on to the hole in the duck's body. The wax spread over the tiny hole and dried as hard as could be! There was no hole there now, and so no water could get in at all.

"Oh, thank you," said the duck. "I hope Janet gives me another chance. If she does, I shall float quite all right."

Then the teddy went to find the lead soldier. He dragged him out of the doll's-house and stood him in front of the toys.

"I'll have your sword, thank you!" he said, and he pulled the little sword from the soldier's hand. "Now you can't do any more damage, you bad-tempered fellow!"

"Please give me my sword back!" cried the soldier in alarm. "A soldier must always carry a sword!"

"Well, you won't," said the teddy, and he threw the sword into the very middle of the nursery fire, where it at once melted! "Now listen to me, soldier – every time you lose your temper we will put you where someone coming into the nursery can tread on you, and you won't like that!"

"I shall run away!" said the soldier. "Wherever you put me I shall just get up and run away!"

"Oh, no you won't!" said the teddy. "Because we shall stick you there with this sealing wax! Aha! It mended the duck's hole and it can keep you stuck to the floor if we want it to! So just you behave yourself in future!"

You wouldn't believe how sweet

tempered the lead soldier was after that. As for the duck, Janet gave her another chance that same night, and she floated beautifully. Janet was so pleased! She still has her in her bath every night – but there's one thing she can't understand.

"I can't understand where the lead soldier's sword has gone," she said to her mother. "It simply isn't anywhere!"

She was right – it simply wasn't anywhere!

# You Mustn't
# Do That!

It happened once that the Lord Rolland bought a beautiful castle for his two children, Prince Peter and Princess Isabel, to live in during the spring and summer. All the people of that place were excited, for they thought it would be very nice for their children to be asked out to tea with a prince and princess.

So the mothers put on their best dresses and went to call, hoping that their children would be chosen to play with Prince Peter and Princess Isabel. The two children were very spoilt, and fond of having their own way, because every boy and girl they had played with had let them do just as they liked – for they were afraid of making a prince and princess angry.

Lord Rolland did not like to see his children so spoilt. "What shall we do about it?" he asked his lovely wife. "Let us be careful what children we choose here to play with Peter and Isabel. We do not want our children spoilt any more than they are. If only we could find some really nice boys and girls, who would help our two to be good and truthful and unselfish. Peter and Isabel have been so spoilt that they are deceitful and very selfish and unkind sometimes."

But there seemed to be no children round about the castle who were any better than Peter and Isabel. In despair Lord Rolland told their nurse that no children at all were to come and play with the prince and princess, for they were behaving even worse than usual! "Let them play in the castle garden by themselves," he said.

But, of course, Peter and Isabel slipped out of the castle garden into a nearby wood every day. It was much more fun in the woods. They ran between the trees, glad to have escaped their nurse.

Presently Peter spied a bird's nest in a tree. "Look!" he called to Isabel. "Here is a nest with four brown eggs in it. Shall we take them home?"

"Oh yes," cried Isabel. "Hand them down to me."

Peter was just putting his hand into the nest when there came the sound of footsteps down the path. He looked to see who it was. He saw two children about his age, poorly but neatly dressed, with merry, smiling faces. One was a boy and one a girl. They were Paul and Anna, children of the wood-cutter and his wife, who lived in a small cottage in the wood.

When Paul saw Peter putting his hand into the nest, he stopped and shouted.

"Hi! What are you doing? You mustn't take birds' eggs! Don't you know that? Come down!"

"Why mustn't we?" asked Isabel, surprised to be spoken to like this.

"Well, would you like to have the beautiful eggs you were so proud of, taken away out of your nest, if you were a bird?" asked Anna. "They belong to the bird, not to you. Our father will never let us take eggs – not even one!"

"Oh," said Peter, jumping to the ground and looking at Paul and Anna. He thought they looked nice children and he felt he would like to play with them. He whispered to Isabel:

"Don't tell these children who we are, Isabel. If they know, they perhaps would be too shy to play with us, for they are only poor children."

"What are you whispering about?" asked Paul. "Don't you know it's rude to whisper when other people are here?"

"No, I didn't know," said Peter. "Don't be angry. Let's be friends. I'd like to play with you."

"But you are rich people's children," said Paul.

"That doesn't matter," said Peter. "Do play!"

So they began to play games and had a wonderful time. Paul wouldn't let Peter cheat and scolded him if he tried to, so that the little prince became ashamed. When Isabel fell down and began to cry although she hadn't hurt herself, Anna laughed.

"Cry-baby!" she said. "You're not hurt. Get up if you want to play. If you don't, we'll play without you."

What a shock for the Princess Isabel, who had only to hurt the tip of her little finger at home, to have everyone flying to her at once! She stared at laughing Anna, and then got up. She did like this little girl so much – and what exciting games these two children knew! How good they were at climbing trees! How well they could jump over the little stream! How exciting it was to hide under a bush and peep out at the rabbits!

The next morning Peter and Isabel met Paul and Anna again. As they were playing, Isabel spied a strange plant growing under a tree. It was a bluebell, but a white one! She was so pleased! She took a piece of wood and began to dig it up to take back to her garden.

"You mustn't do that!" cried Anna, running up. "The flowers here belong to everybody – you must leave them for people to enjoy. Why should you have them, Isabel? Don't be selfish."

Isabel went red and stopped digging up the root. She ran to join the game and thought about what Anna had said. After all – why should she have the lovely flower in her own little garden just for herself to see? It belonged to everyone!

That day Peter and Isabel had brought their lunch with them to have a picnic and so had the wood-cutter's children. The four of them sat down to eat sandwiches, apples and chocolate. All the crust had been cut off Peter's sandwiches and Isabel's, and they were neat, small and trim – but Paul and Anna had big,

crusty sandwiches. Peter and Isabel thought they looked lovely, and they wished theirs were the same. After they had finished their meal Peter threw his sandwich paper away and left his apple core on the grass. So did Isabel.

"You mustn't do that!" cried Paul, quite shocked. "Pick up that paper, Peter, and the apple core – and the chocolate paper, Isabel. You can't spoil the woods like that – why, anyone might come along and picnic here tomorrow, and think how spoiled the place would be! You are selfish!"

"Don't be cross," said Isabel, slipping her hand into Paul's hand. "We'll pick up everything and take it back home with us."

They did and when they popped the paper into the wastepaper basket at home, Peter looked at Isabel and laughed. "I shall call those children the 'Mustn't Do Thats'," he said. "They are always saying that to us!"

For many days the four children played happily together. Then one day Peter

brought with him a bag of such beautiful chocolates that Paul and Anna cried out in astonishment. "Wherever did you get them?" said Paul.

"Don't tell anyone, will you," said Peter. "I took them out of a box that my mother had. She'll never miss them!"

Paul and Anna stared at Peter in horror. "But you mustn't do that!" they cried, both together. "Why, that's stealing! And from your own mother too! How ever can you do such a thing? Don't you love your mother? Why, we could never never take anything without asking our mother first!"

"Our mother wouldn't mind," said Peter, red-faced and sulky.

"Well, if she wouldn't mind, why didn't you ask her instead of taking the chocolates behind her back?" cried Paul at once. "I think you are horrid, Peter. You are always doing things like this. You aren't nice to know. We won't play with you any more!"

With that Paul and Anna ran off home and left Peter and Isabel by themselves. They were both red, angry and ashamed. "Nasty children!" said Isabel, tears trickling down her cheeks. "I don't like them."

"Oh, yes you do," said Peter, taking her hand. "You know, Isabel – I think

*we* are the nasty children, don't you?"
Let's go and put these chocolates back.
We'll come here tomorrow as usual, and
tell Paul and Anna what we've done and
say we're sorry. They are the nicest
children we've ever known, and we must
keep them for our friends. I'd like to be
like them, you know – always so straight,
and kind and happy. It's no wonder we
like them!"

Now the next morning, as Peter and
Isabel were slipping out of the castle
garden as usual, the Lord Rolland saw
them. "Little monkeys!" he thought.
"Now where are they going? I'll follow
them and see."

So he followed them until they met
Paul and Anna. He saw Peter and Isabel
run up to the wood-cutter's children and
take their hands.

"Paul! Anna!" cried Peter. "We put
back those chocolates we stole. We'll
never do such a thing like that again.
Please go on being friends with us. We do
like you so much."

"Well, we don't like you," said Paul,

pushing away Peter's hand. "We think you are untruthful, unkind, mean and cowardly. We don't want to know you."

"You horrid boy!" said Peter, fiercely. "Do you know who we are? We are Prince Peter and Princess Isabel. How dare you say things like that to us! You ought to be proud that we want to be friends with you."

Paul and Anna stared at the children in surprise. "Well – we're not proud!" said Paul. "And it doesn't make any difference at all who you are. An honest and kind wood-cutter is better than a mean and selfish prince. Goodbye!"

Just as the children turned to go, Lord Rolland stepped out from the trees where he had been standing, listening in surprise to all this. Peter and Isabel were frightened, for they knew they were supposed to be in the garden. Paul and Anna looked up, wondering who the grand man was.

"I am these children's father," said Lord Rolland. "I want to ask you a favour, Paul and Anna. Will you try to

forget what spoilt children Peter and
Isabel are, and help them to be nicer?
You are quite right in what you say – an
honest and kindly wood-cutter is better
than a mean and selfish prince. Well,
since these children like you so much,
what about seeing if you can help them to
be honest and kindly like yourselves?"

"Oh, Paul, Anna, do be friends again," begged Isabel, slipping her hand into Paul's. "We do like you so much. We'll do anything you say if only you'll play with us again."

"Paul, let's be friends with them," begged Anna too, who was very kind-hearted. "They have tried to be better, you know. They put those chocolates back, and they are sorry. I expect they've just been spoilt. They are nice underneath."

"All right," said Paul, holding out his hand to Peter. "But mind, Peter – I am not being friends with you just because you are a prince. I shall still tell you if you mustn't do things!"

Lord Rolland went to see the wood-cutter, and arranged that Paul and Anna should have lessons with Peter and Isabel and play with them each day. Twice a week they had tea at the castle and once a week Paul and Anna took the little prince and princess home to tea. How they loved it all! And how much nicer Peter and Isabel became before many

weeks had passed. You wouldn't have known them for the same children!

All the rich mothers and fathers who lived nearby were amazed when they heard that Lord Rolland had chosen the wood-cutter's children as friends for his own children. "Whatever can he see in children like that!" they marvelled. "What a strange idea!"

But it wasn't so strange, really, was it? I think he was wise to choose children who knew what honesty and kindness meant, don't you – because they are the things that really matter!

# The Three
# Chocolate Bears

Once upon a time Auntie Sarah bought Jimmy, Jane and Joseph three chocolate bears. They were fine bears, with long noses and big fat legs, made of the loveliest milk chocolate you can imagine.

But Mother wouldn't let the children eat the bears, because she said it would spoil their lunches.

"Well, where shall we put them, then?" said Auntie Sarah. "It's such a terribly hot day that they are sure to melt."

"Put them in the fridge," said Mother. "They will keep nice and hard there."

So the three bears were put into the fridge. Ooh, it was cold! It was freezing cold there! The bears began to shiver and shake.

"I say! This is a horrible place to put

us!" said the bears. "They must think we are polar bears! We shall be lumps of ice soon."

"I'm going to jump out of here as soon as anyone opens the door," said the biggest bear. "I can't stand it."

He didn't have to wait very long. Mother came to get out the butter, and as soon as she opened the fridge out jumped all the three chocolate bears and ran down the kitchen as fast as they could.

"Ooh, my goodness, what's that?" cried Mother, in a fright. "Mice, it must be mice! Now how in the world did they get in there?"

The three bears chuckled to hear themselves called mice. They ran to the boiler and sat down by it.

But Spot, the dog, was lying asleep nearby, and he smelled them in his dream. He woke up, and sniffed. When he saw the chocolate bears he ran to them to eat them. In a terrible fright they rushed out of the kitchen door into the garden. They crept under the back gate, and ran down the path. Spot couldn't follow them because he was too big to get under the gate, and he couldn't open it by himself.

"I still feel very cold," said the middle bear, shivering. "If only we could have stayed by that warm boiler!"

"Look! There's a big lump of feathers lying in that ditch!" said the smallest bear. "Feathers are warm. Let's go and cuddle into them."

So they ran over to the big lump of

84

feathers and burrowed right into them. Ooh, they were warm! The bears stopped shivering and began to feel happier.

But, oh my goodness, the lump of feathers was a sleeping hen! When she felt the chocolate bears burrowing into her feathers, she woke up and looked quite startled. Then she suddenly stood up.

Out dropped the bears with a thud, and the hen clucked in fright. She pecked the ear of the biggest bear and then ran away, squawking loudly.

The three bears were so frightened
that they began to shiver again.

"That was a narrow escape," they said.
"Come on, let's find somewhere else."

On they went, and soon came to what
looked like a big pink wall. They touched
it. It was very warm.

"Let's lean up against this," said the
middle bear. "It's nice and hot."

So they did – but they hadn't been
there very long before the wall shook
and shivered and a piggy voice said, "My
gracious, something's tickling me
dreadfully!"

And it was a pig! Yes, a fat pink pig
lying down in his sty. How scared the
three bears were!

"This is dreadful!" they said, scurrying away. "We were nearly eaten then."

They rushed out of the sty, and came out into a little lane. The sun shone down there and the lane was hot.

"Let's sit down here," said the biggest bear, sleepily. "That must be a great big fire burning up in the sky. It will warm us nicely. The grass is so soft here, too."

So they sat down and went to sleep in the sun – and, oh dear, dear me – the sun was so terribly hot that they began to melt. And when they woke up they had melted all away into three little brown chocolate puddles in the grass!

"I can't get up," said the first bear.

"I haven't any legs," said the second bear.

"I'm a p-p-p-puddle!" whispered the third bear.

And then a grey donkey came by and licked them all up. "Funny sort of puddles those were!" said he. "I wish I could find some more like them!"

But he couldn't!

# The Toys' Great Adventure

Jack and Ann were turning out their toy-cupboard. It was nearly Christmas time, and they knew they would soon have plenty of new toys.

"We simply must make room for them," said Ann. "We must throw out any toys we don't want. What about this car, Jack?"

"It was very nice when it was new," he said. "But it won't run now because of its bent wheel."

"Then we'll throw it away," said Ann, and she put it into the wastepaper basket.

"Oh look – here's the little rag-doll," said Ann, suddenly. "I haven't played with her for ages. Her black hair is very untidy – it looks like a mop!"

So into the basket went Mopsy the rag-doll. She fell beside the toy car.

"I used to love this clockwork man," said Jack. "But we lost his key ages ago, so he can't walk now." So into the basket went Mr Click, the clockwork man.

"Any more to throw away?" said Ann.

"What about this tiny bear?" said Jack, holding him up. "We called him Biggy Bear because he was so small. Do you remember?"

"Yes," said Ann, taking the little bear. "It's a shame, but he's very dirty, and he's lost an eye."

So Biggy went into the wastepaper basket too!

"There!" said Ann, looking into the empty toy-cupboard. "That's everything. Let's clean the shelves and put back the things we are keeping. We'll have a whole shelf empty for our new toys."

They worked hard till bedtime. Their mother was very pleased when she came to take them to bed.

"Well done!" she said. "I'll take this rubbish down to the kitchen. We can put it in the dustbin tomorrow."

Mother took the basket of old toys down to the kitchen and then went off to see the children into bed. The kitchen cat sniffed in the basket to see if there was anything to eat there. But there wasn't.

"Just a lot of dirty old toys," said the cat to herself, as she curled up on the kitchen chair.

After everyone had gone to bed that night, everything was dark and quiet in the kitchen. Not a sound was to be heard except for the gentle snoring of the tabby cat. Suddenly the cat pricked up her ears. She had heard something. Was it a mouse? No, the noise was coming from the wastepaper basket! Mopsy, Mr Click and Biggy Bear slowly sat up and peeped over the edge of the wastepaper basket. The moonlight shone on them from the kitchen window and they looked at one another dolefully.

"Dustbin for us tomorrow," said Mopsy.

"Don't you believe it!" said Mr Click. "I'm not staying here to be popped into the dustbin!"

"But you can't go far without being wound up," said Mopsy. Mr Click looked very gloomy.

"Yes, you're right. I can walk a few steps and then I come to a stop. What a pity! It would have been fun to run away, and take you and Biggy Bear with me, Mopsy."

"Shh! Here comes the cat!" said Mopsy, and they all slid down into the basket again. Mopsy fell next to the toy car. Suddenly she had an idea.

"Mr Click!" she whispered. "Do you think the key to the clockwork car would fit you? Shall I try?"

"If you like," said Mr Click. "But Ann and Jack tried hundreds of other keys and not one worked."

The toys waited until the cat had gone back to sleep. Then Mopsy tried the car key.

"It fits!" said Biggy, excited.

"But it won't turn to wind me up – you just see!" said Mr Click, gloomily.

"Mr Click! It *does* turn!" cried Mopsy. "You can walk again."

"Well, what a lovely surprise!" said Mr Click, smiling. "Mopsy – Biggy – oh, will you come with me? We'll run away and

find a dear little house somewhere. We won't go into the dustbin!"

"Yes. We'd love to come," said Mopsy and Biggy.

"Wait," said Mr Click. "My key's dropped out. It's fallen to the bottom of the basket. I shall lose it!"

Mopsy scrabbled about in the basket and found the key. "I shall tie the key to the strings of my apron," she said. "Now we can't possibly lose it!"

"Let's go now!" said Biggy, jigging up and down.

"Wait," said Mr Click suddenly. "I've had an idea!"

"What is it?" said Biggy Bear and Mopsy.

"Let's take the old toy car with us," said Mr Click. "We could go for miles in that."

They pulled the car out of the basket on to the kitchen floor. "See – the wheel is bent, but I can easily straighten that," said Mr Click.

Soon the wheel was quite straight again, and the car could run along well, though it was a bit wobbly. Then Mr Click straightened the squashed-in roof.

"There!" he said. "It's mended! I'll drive. I used to drive this car round the playroom before it was broken. Get in beside me, Biggy. You get in the back, Mopsy."

The others got in, feeling very excited. Then Mopsy thought of something. "How can we get out of the house? The door is locked."

"Oh, I've thought of that," said Mr Click. "We'll just drive out of the cat's door!"

And that is what they did! With a clickety-click, out they went through the cat's little door. They were out in the garden now. The little car was wobbly, and Biggy and Mopsy clutched the sides hard as they rattled over stones in the gravel path.

The car came to a stop at the end of the garden. Mopsy took the key off her apron string and gave it to Mr Click to wind up the car again. Then she tied it safely on to her apron string once more.

"We must find somewhere to live," said Mopsy to Mr Click. "I'm a very good cook. I can look after you both very well indeed."

"Yes, do let's find somewhere," said Biggy Bear. "Somewhere with a tiny garden. I'm such a good gardener, you know, I love digging."

"Right," said Mr Click. "We'll find a nice little house with a tiny garden for Biggy to dig in. I'd rather like a garage for the car, too. I can look after that. I'm good with cars."

But it wasn't easy to find a house. They looked and looked, but there didn't seem to be any about at all.

"I'm so sleepy," said Mopsy at last. "Can we sleep in the car tonight and look for a house in the morning?"

So Mr Click parked the car under a hedge and they all fell fast asleep. In the morning, a robin woke them up by singing loudly in their ears.

"Hello, Robin!" said Mopsy. "You don't know where we could find a little house with a tiny garden and a garage, do you?"

"Ask Tickles the elf!" said the robin. "She lives in that tree."

He flew to the tree and knocked on it with his beak. A little door opened and Tickles the elf looked out. She was small and pretty and had a cloud of golden hair.

"What is it you want?" she said. "A house? Oh yes, I know where there is one to let. Come in and have breakfast with me, then I'll show you the house."

So they all went into Tickles' little round room inside the tree and had a delicious breakfast.

"Now come with me and I'll show you the house!" said Tickles. "You'll love it!"

The house was a very large toadstool with a small door in the stalk. Inside, a winding staircase went up to a big room at the top of the toadstool. There were three windows in the roof, so the room was full of light.

"It's lovely!" said Mopsy in delight. "And it's furnished too. What dear little chairs and tables!"

"Is there a garage for the car?" asked Mr Click.

"Is there a teeny-weeny garden?" asked Biggy.

"No," said Tickles. "It's just a house."

"Well, we'll take it and move in," said Mopsy, sitting down in the chairs to see if they were comfortable.

"Listen!" said Tickles, suddenly. "Oh dear! Whatever shall we do? He's back again!"

"Who's back?" said Mopsy, Mr Click and Biggy Bear.

"The old black horse who lives in this field," said Tickles. "He's been away for ages. He's got great big feet. Once he even knocked down a toadstool house."

"Quick! Get out!" shouted Mr Click, as the heavy footsteps came nearer and nearer.

*Clip-clop, clip-clop! Hrrrumph!* Tickles and the others almost fell down the stairs in their hurry. They reached the safety of

Tickles' tree just in time, watching in horror as one of the horse's enormous hooves knocked down the dear little toadstool house. Mopsy and Tickles screamed.

"It's broken! It's ruined!" cried Tickles. The top had broken off the stalk, and tiny chairs lay on the grass. Mopsy began to cry.

"Never mind. It didn't have a garage," said Mr Click, trying to comfort her.

"And there wasn't even a teeny-weeny garden," said Biggy Bear.

"I don't mind about those," sobbed Mopsy. "It was the house I wanted. Now we'll have to find another."

"Well, wind me up, and we'll go off in the car again," said Mr Click. "Cheer up, Mopsy. I'll find a beautiful house soon."

They said goodbye to poor Tickles, climbed into the car, and drove off. They all felt very sad. It had been such a dear little house. Would they ever find another?

They drove about all that day and the next. They had meals with all sorts of

people, who were very kind to them. A family of rabbits gave them a salad supper. A little green goblin shared his breakfast with them. Two pixies took them into their home under the hedge and gave them lunch. But they didn't find a house.

Then, that afternoon, they came to a garden. There was a big house there, rather like the one that Ann and Jack lived in, with a wide veranda. Mr Click drove the little car on to the veranda to get out of the rain. In the corner was a big box of toy bricks! It was partly covered by a dirty old cloth. Dust and cobwebs lay on both box and cloth.

"Look! These bricks must have been forgotten!" said Mr Click. "No one has used them for ages. Let's build a house with them!"

"What a lovely idea!" said Mopsy. "Do you know how to build a house, Mr Click?"

"I think so," he replied. "Biggy can help me. We'll build a house in the corner here. We can build a garage, too."

"What about a garden?" asked Biggy.

"Oh, you and your garden!" said Mr Click. "You can't build gardens, Biggy. You have to make one. Come and help me to carry these bricks."

Mr Click was very busy as they built the house. He ran about here and there, and Mopsy had to wind him up dozens of times. Two windows went in, a back door and a front door, and steps up to the front. And then, the roof went on! There

were three chimneys so they each put
one on. Then they opened the front door
and walked inside their new house.

"It's lovely," said Mopsy, happily. "We
shall have to buy some furniture, but we
can sleep on the floor till we have beds."

"I'm so tired I could sleep anywhere,"
said Biggy Bear yawning.

Next morning, they left the house,
shutting the front door behind them,
and went to find some breakfast. A little
mouse they met kindly gave them some
cheese and a bit of pie. People were really
very kind to them. They told the mouse
about their new house.

"Come and see it," said Mopsy. So they
took the little mouse to the veranda. But,
oh dear, what a dreadful shock they had
when they got there!

The house wasn't there any longer!
All the bricks were packed away neatly in
the box once more.

"So they did belong to somebody," said
Mopsy, sadly. "And the Somebody has
come along and unbuilt our house, and
packed it all away. It's no good building it

again. We'll have to find another!"

"I know where there's a house!" said the little mouse, suddenly. "It might just do nicely for you. But it's only got one room – though it's a very big one!"

He led them down the garden, with Mr Click bumping along in the car behind him. They came to a small wooden building, with a very large open doorway.

"It's a funny place," said Mopsy, peering inside. "A doorway and no door to shut! And not a single window to let in light and air! I don't think I like it very much."

"Why is there all this straw on the floor?" said Biggy Bear. "It's very prickly."

"There's no garage," said Mr Click. "But this one room is so large that the car could live here with us."

"There's no garden, either," said Biggy.

"You could perhaps dig a bit of the ground outside the house for a garden," said the little mouse.

"Yes, I suppose I could," said Biggy. "Who does the house belong to, mouse?"

"I don't know who it belongs to," said the mouse. "I've only just come to this place myself. I should move in if I were you, before anyone else does."

"Right," said Mr Click. "Help me in with the car, please, Biggy."

They were all very tired when they had dragged the car inside. They sat down to get their breath. Mopsy leaned against Mr Click, and Biggy leaned against the car. In a few minutes they were all asleep!

Suddenly a great big head looked into the doorway and big panting breaths filled the air. Mopsy screamed.

"What's all this?" said a deep wuffy voice. "Who are you? What are you doing in my kennel?"

There was a long silence. A kennel! So that's what the wooden house was. No wonder it had no door and no windows. It belonged to a dog.

"We must go," said Mr Click, in a small voice. "Sorry, Mr Dog! We came in here not knowing it belonged to you. We'll go!"

And very sadly Mr Click, Mopsy and Biggy Bear dragged out the car, wound it up, got into it and set off.

"We must try and find another house," said poor Mopsy. "How unlucky we are!"

The car chugged on for a long, long way. It stopped by a signpost. Mopsy leaned out to read it.

"To Pixie-Land," she read. "Well, we might as well go there. There might be an empty house there."

So on they went. They knew they were in Pixie-Land because of all the little folk they met. But they couldn't find a house even there! There was only an empty rabbit-hole to let, and they had to take that. It was very sad because it wasn't a house, there was no garage, and, of course, not even a garden.

Not far off was a beautiful house, big and full of lovely furniture, with a garage full of cars, and a perfectly lovely garden. And it was empty!

"It belongs to Princess Starlight," said Mopsy. "She is away ill. It's such a shame. All the furniture is getting dusty, and the cars need cleaning and the garden is a mass of weeds."

"Perhaps we could clean everything

up a little," said Mr Click. "I'd love to
polish those cars."

So, when their work was finished each
day, the three friends climbed over the
wall of the Princess's house and went to
work there. Biggy was so happy digging
and weeding. He sang in a little growly
voice all the time. Mopsy climbed in
through the kitchen window. She found
mops and brooms and dusters and
started to clean the house.

"If I can't have a house of my own to
clean, I'll clean somebody else's," she
thought.

As for Mr Click, he was so happy that he whistled loudly as he washed and polished each car.

They were very happy in their secret work.

"The house looks beautiful inside!" said Mopsy.

"The garden is spick and span and full of flowers!" said Biggy Bear, who looked dirtier than ever.

"The cars shine as if they were new," said Mr Click.

And then something happened! One day when they went to the house they found the gates and the front door open, and all the windows were thrown open too! They stood and stared.

"Her Highness the Princess Starlight is expected back today," said the postman, going in with a lot of letters. "Somebody is getting the place ready for her."

"No more cleaning up that lovely house!" said Mopsy, sadly.

"No more digging in the garden," said Biggy.

110

"No more looking after those beautiful cars," said Mr Click. "Come on – we'd better go home."

"I do hope the Princess won't mind that we've been in her house and garden," said Mopsy, alarmed. "I don't think anyone ever saw us. But you never know!"

The next day there was a big notice up on the wall of the nearby village.

WILL THOSE WHO HAVE BEEN IN THE HOUSE AND GARAGE AND GARDEN BELONGING TO PRINCESS STARLIGHT PLEASE GO TO HER AT ONCE.

"Will she punish us?" said Mopsy, looking frightened.

"Don't let's go," said Biggy.

"We must go," said Mr Click. "We can't be cowards. I expect all that will happen will be that we'll be sent away in disgrace."

They went to see the Princess Starlight. She was very lovely. They bowed low before her.

"We're the ones who came and trespassed," said Mr Click, humbly. "You see, Your Highness, we so badly wanted a house with a garden and garage for ourselves, but we couldn't find one, so we sort of borrowed yours. But we didn't live here."

"And we didn't do any harm," said

Biggy. "We just looked after everything."

"And I didn't break anything, honestly," said Mopsy. "I do hope you won't punish us too much."

The Princess looked at the little clockwork man with his smily face, at little black-haired Mopsy, and the dirty one-eyed bear. She smiled sweetly.

"I hope you won't find your punishment too hard," she said. "I am going to make you come and live here! Mopsy, you are to be my housekeeper. Biggy, you shall be my head gardener. Mr Click, you are to be my chauffeur, and drive me anywhere I want to go."

"Oh!" said Mopsy. "OH! That's no punishment. It's wonderful! I don't know what to say!"

"And as soon as I can, I shall have a little house built especially for you," said the Princess. "Can you move in today? I was so pleased to find the house and the garden and the cars looking so lovely when I came home! Thank you all so much."

Well, Mr Click, Mopsy and Biggy moved in that very day. Biggy had a bath and came out clean. The Princess gave him a new eye and he looked really handsome. Then the Princess combed Mopsy's hair and tied it in two bunches. She looked very pretty.

That's a year ago now. The Princess kept her word and built them a tiny

house with a tiny garden and a tiny garage for the old clockwork car. They are all very happy indeed, and Biggy grows bigger cabbages than any other gardener there!

"This is better than going into the dustbin!" Mopsy often says. "Whatever would Jack and Ann say if they could see us now?"

They would be surprised, wouldn't they?

# The Magic
# Pinny-minny Flower

Too-Thin the Magician was making a new spell. He had nearly everything he wanted for it – a bowl of moonlight, a skein of spider's thread, six golden dewdrops, two hairs from a rabbit's tail, and many other things – but there was still one thing he hadn't got.

"I must have a blue pinny-minny flower. Now I wonder where I can get one."

He went out into his garden to think about it. He walked round and round it, up and down the paths, and thought hard. The beds were full of spring daffodils, but Too-Thin didn't notice them. A freckled thrush was singing a new song in the almond tree, but Too-Thin didn't hear it. He didn't even know it was springtime, for he didn't care about things like that.

He frowned and thought harder than ever. He really must have a blue pinny-minny flower, but where to get one he couldn't think.

"I must pin a notice to my gate, and offer a reward to anyone who can bring me what I want," said the magician at last. So he wrote out a notice and pinned it on his gate. This is what it said:

SIX SACKS OF GOLD WILL BE GIVEN TO ANYONE WHO BRINGS A BLUE PINNY-MINNY FLOWER TO TOO-THIN THE MAGICIAN.

Then Too-Thin went indoors and began to stir the dewdrops in the bowl of moonlight.

Now many people passed by Too-Thin's gate and read the notice. Nobody knew where to get a blue pinny-minny flower at all. Many of them wrote to witches they knew, and to goblins who lived in mountain caves, asking if they could find a blue pinny-minny flower – but no one could.

One day Higgledy, a tiny cobbler pixie, passed by. He was very poor and lived in a tumbledown cottage with no garden. He often used to peep over the wall that ran round Too-Thin's garden, and look at the rows of daffodils there. He wished he could have a garden like it and grow snowdrops, crocuses and daffodils, and roses in the summertime.

Higgledy read the notice and then his eyes opened in surprise.

"Surely Too-Thin does not mean this," he said. He climbed up to the top of the wall and sat there, looking into the magician's garden. He looked over to the

118

doorway of the house, for he had often seen a tiny plant growing in the stones of the pathway there.

The plant was still there, and Higgledy stared in astonishment.

"Why, there's the pinny-minny plant still growing outside the magician's own door," he said to himself. "I've often seen it when I've looked over the wall. Can it be that the magician doesn't know it's there?"

He jumped over the wall and ran to the door. Yes, it was a pinny-minny plant right enough. Just as he was thinking of knocking at the door and telling the magician, Too-Thin came out, looking rather cross, for he was in a bad temper.

"Now then, now then," he said. "What do you want? Have you come about the eggs?"

"No," said Higgledy, 'I'm not the egg-man. I've come about the pinny-minny plant."

"Where is it?" cried the magician. "Have you brought it with you?"

"No," said Higgledy, "you see—"

"Oh, you stupid creature!" cried Too-Thin. "Go and get it at once. Is it in someone's garden? Well go and pick it! You can pay them for it with the gold I shall give you in return."

Higgledy laughed. He suddenly bent down and picked a blue pinny-minny flower from the plant by his foot. Then he waved it in the magician's face.

"Here it is!" he cried. "You pass it every day when you walk into the garden, and never see it! Oh, Too-Thin, you may be clever at spells, but you are very stupid at

other things! Why don't you use your eyes?"

Too-Thin stared in amazement. Why, here was the very flower he had wanted for so long! And to think it grew in his very own garden and he hadn't seen it! He went very red, and took it from Higgledy.

"You shall have the six sacks of gold," he said, "even though the plant grew in my own garden – but you must promise not to tell anyone where you found it, for I don't want to be laughed at."

"I promise," said Higgledy. Then the magician sent him to fetch a barrow in which he could wheel home his gold, and while Higgledy was gone Too-Thin looked round his garden and saw it for the first time.

"I really must use my eyes more!" he said. "Why, those daffodils are beautiful! And listen to that thrush! Whatever is the use of being a clever magician if I forget to look at daffodils? Well, well, Higgledy has earned his gold, for he has opened my eyes for me!"

Higgledy was so pleased with his good fortune. He bought a beautiful little cottage with a garden and married a nice little wife. And what do you think he called his new cottage? Why, Pinny-Minny Cottage! So if ever you come across it, you'll know who lives there!

# Look Out, Busy-Body!

Busy-Body the elf was always poking his nose into everything. He knew everyone's business, and told everyone's secrets. He was a perfect little nuisance.

He peeped here and poked there. If Dame Twig had a new hen, he knew all about it. If Mr Round had a new hat he knew exactly what it was like, and where it was from. He was a real little busybody, so his name was a very good one.

One day Madam Soapsuds came to live in Chestnut Village, where Busy-Body's cottage was. She arrived in a small van labelled "Laundry Goods. With Very Great Care". She wouldn't let the removal men unpack the van, telling them she wished to do it herself.

Busy-Body was very curious, of course.

Why should she want to unpack the van herself? Was there something magic in it that she didn't want anyone else to see? He decided to hide in the front garden, and watch till Madam Soapsuds took out whatever was in that little van.

That night, before the moon was up, Madam Soapsuds came out into the garden, and went over to the van. But before she opened the door, she said a little magic rhyme:

"If anyone is hiding,
They must go a-riding,
On this witch's stick."

She tossed an old broomstick on to the floor. Though he tried to escape it, it swept poor Busy-Body out from behind the bush where he was hiding, and carried him up into the air, feeling very frightened indeed.

"Ho, ho!" said Madam Soapsuds. "I had an idea you were trying to poke your silly little nose into my business, Busy-Body. Better stay away from me. I keep my secrets!"

So, while Busy-Body rose high above the village, Madam Soapsuds quickly and quietly unpacked that secret little van, and nobody saw her. Busy-Body had a dreadful night. It was windy and cold. He wasn't used to riding broomsticks. It was most uncomfortable, and very jerky, so he had to cling on tightly. He felt sure the stick was jerking on purpose.

When the sun came up, the broomstick landed, leaving Busy-Body stiff, cold and very angry. How dare Madam Soapsuds treat him like that! He'd find out all her secrets, no matter what!

Madam Soapsuds told everyone what

had happened and they laughed. "How do you like riding at night?" they teased.

Busy-Body scowled. He hoped no one would like Madam Soapsuds. But they did like her, and very much too. She ran a fine laundry. They could take a bag of washing to her in the morning and have it back, washed, mangled, dried and ironed at teatime. It was really wonderful.

She wouldn't let anyone watch her at work. "No," she said, "I like to work alone, thank you."

"She's got some special magic secret at work," said Busy-Body to everyone. "She couldn't possibly do all that washing herself. Why, she had seven bags of dirty linen to wash today, and a pile of blankets from Dame Twig. And hey presto! By teatime they were all clean, dry and ironed!"

Busy-Body puzzled day and night over her secret. It might be magic machinery, or hundreds of tiny imp servants that had been in that van.

Madam Soapsuds had a big room in

her house that nobody went into, called her Washing Room. Strange noises came from it, clankings, splashings and bumpings. "Can't I just peek inside and see?" asked her friend, Dame Twig. But Madam Soapsuds shook her head.

"No. It would be dangerous. Not even I go into that room. I just take the dirty linen in there, shut the door and leave it. At teatime I open the door, and there it is, clean, dry and ironed, piled neatly for me to take."

"Extraordinary," said Dame Twig. "Well, Madam Soapsuds, watch out for Busy-Body. He'll poke his nose into that room if he possibly can."

"He'll be sorry if he does," said Madam Soapsuds.

Busy-Body certainly meant to find out the secret of that Washing Room. He watched Madam Soapsuds from the window of his cottage opposite every day. He knew that she did not often go out during the week, but on Saturdays she went to visit her sister in the next village for the whole day.

"That's the day for me to go to her house," thought the elf. "She's away all day! I can get in through her window, because she always leaves it a little bit open. Oo, Madam Soapsuds, I'll soon know your secret and tell everyone! I'm sure it's one you're ashamed of, or you wouldn't hide it so carefully!"

That Saturday, Madam Soapsuds put on her best bonnet and shawl as usual, took a basket of goodies, and caught the bus to the next village.

Busy-Body waited until the bus had left. He crept out of his cottage, and went round to the back of Madam Soapsuds' house. No one was about.

The sitting-room window was open as usual. He slid it up, and jumped inside. From the Washing Room he could hear curious sounds:

*Slishy-sloshy, splish-splash-splosh. Creak-clank, creak! Flap-flap-flap! Drippitty, drip! Bump-bump-bump!*

He stood and listened to the noises, filled with curiosity. He must peep inside and see what was happening.

The door was shut tight. He turned the handle and the door opened. A puff of steam came out in his face. Busy-Body carefully put his head round the door, but he couldn't see a thing because it was so steamy. He listened to the odd noises. Whatever could be making them?

He went cautiously inside. The door slammed shut behind him. Busy-Body turned in fright and tried to open it, but he couldn't. Ooooh!

The steam cleared a little and he saw that the room was full of tubs of water, swirling steam, mangles that swung their rollers round fast and creaked and clanked, and hot irons that bumped their way over tables on which clothes were spreading themselves ready to be pressed.

No one was there. Everything was working at top speed by itself. The soap in the tubs made a tremendous lather, the scrubbing-brushes worked hard, the mangles pressed the water from clothes, the whirling fan that dried them rushed busily round and round up in the ceiling.

Busy-Body felt scared. He had never

seen so much magic at work.

He felt himself pushed towards one of the tubs. In he went, *splash*, into the hot water. A large piece of soap ran over him and a big frothy lather appeared. He spluttered as soap went in his eyes and nose.

"Stop! Stop!" begged Busy-Body. But the magic couldn't stop. It was set to go, and go on it had to. Besides, it didn't often have a real person to wash, mangle and iron!

Poor Busy-Body was soaked in tub after tub, soaped and re-soaped, lathered, and scrubbed till he felt as if he was nothing but a bit of rag.

He was whizzed over to one of the mangles whose rollers were turning busily, squeezing the water out of the flattened clothes. Look out, Busy-Body!

He just managed to fling himself down below the mangle before he was put in between the rollers.

He crawled into a corner, and wept.

Why had he bothered about Madam Soapsuds' horrible secret?

A tub rolled near him, splashing him with cold water. Then he was flung up to the ceiling, where he was hung on a wire to dry in the wind made by the magic fan, and then thrown back down to the floor.

Look out, Busy-Body! You're near the magic irons! *Wheeeeee!* He was up on the ironing table, and a hot iron ran over his leg! Busy-Body squealed, and leaped off the table. Into a tub of hot water he went this time, and a big scrubbing-brush began to scrub him in delight. Then he was flung into a tub of cold water and rinsed well.

"I've never been so wet in my life! I've never had to much soap in my mouth and nose and eyes! Oh, how can I get away?"

It was lucky for Busy-Body that Madam Soapsuds came home early that day, or he would certainly have been mangled and ironed sooner or later. But suddenly the door opened, and a voice said:

"I have come for you, clothes!"

At once the clean, dry, mangled, ironed clothes made neat piles by the door – and on top poor Busy-Body was flung, wet and dripping!

"Good gracious! What's this?" said Madam Soapsuds, in surprise. "You, Busy-Body! Serves you right for peeping and prying. You're not dry, mangled or ironed. Go back and be done properly."

"No, no!" squealed Busy-Body, afraid.

"Let me go. Please let me go!"

Madam Soapsuds got hold of him. He was dripping from head to foot.

"Maybe I'll peg you up on my line in the garden instead," she said.

And to Busy-Body's shame and horror, she pegged him firmly up on her clothes-line by the seat of his trousers – and there he swung in the wind, unable to get away.

Everyone came to look and laugh.

"He poked his nose into what didn't concern him," said Madam Soapsuds. "He's got a lot of secrets to tell. But if he tells them he'll go back into my Washing Room to learn a few more!"

Busy-Body was so ashamed and unhappy that he cried tears into the puddle made by his dripping clothes.

Nobody felt very sorry for him. Busy-bodies are always punished by themselves in the end!

"Now you can go," Madam Soapsuds said at last, unpegging him. "And what are you going to do, Busy-Body? Are you going to run round telling my secrets?"

No. Busy-Body wasn't going to do anything of the sort. He didn't even want to think of that awful Washing Room. So he tried not to.

But he can't help dreaming about it, and when the neighbours hear him yelling at night, they laugh and say:

"He thinks he's in that Washing Room again. Poor Busy-Body!"

# Ginger Really is
# a Help

Bobby took his kite out into the garden to fly it. "It's such a lovely windy day," he said. "Kite, you will fly right up to the clouds today."

He unwound some of the ball of string. The cat next door, who was sitting on the wall, saw him, and jumped down at once – it loved playing with string.

"Now, you go away, Ginger," said Bobby, who wasn't fond of animals. "I don't want you tangling up my string and messing it about. Cats can't help fly kites, so go away."

But the cat wouldn't go away. It waited till Bobby had put the ball of string on the ground for a minute, while he went to look at his kite – and then it pounced on the string. Bobby gave a shout.

"Didn't I tell you not to play with my string! Go back over the wall, Ginger. You are a nuisance of a cat. Last week you sat on my garden just when my seeds were coming up – and this week you tangle my kite-string!"

The cat leaped away at Bobby's shout. But it sat and watched while the boy threw the kite into the wind and then let out some of the string.

"Up you go, kite, up you go!" cried Bobby in delight. The wind was very strong and the kite pulled hard. Bobby let out the string as fast as he could.

But suddenly a knot came and he looked down at the string. "Bother! Now I'll have to undo a knot. Wait a bit, kite, don't pull so!"

But the kite wanted to go much higher and it gave such a sudden pull that Bobbie felt the ball of string jerked right out of his hands! It fell to the ground, unravelled a little – and then, as the wind took the kite along, the ball of string rolled down the garden, bumping along at top speed!

"Oh stop! Oh, I'll lose my kite! Mum, I've dropped the ball of string! Oh stop, string!" cried Bobby.

But the kite, feeling nice and free, was glad to fly off in the wind, dragging its string behind it! The ball came to the wall and ran up it. It caught on a rambling rose and stuck there for a few minutes. Bobby ran to it and almost grabbed it – but it got free and hopped right over the wall, dragged by the flying kite!

"Oh dear! Now the string has gone into the field!" shouted Bobby. "I've got to go over the wall too – I'll never catch it! I'll lose my kite!"

Ginger the cat was watching everything in great surprise. What was happening? He saw the ball of string rolling down the garden – he saw it swing up the wall – and get caught on a thorn. Then over the wall it went and disappeared.

Ginger was puzzled. Where had it gone? Had it suddenly come alive? What fun to chase it! Bobby was chasing it, so why shouldn't he?

And away went Ginger down the garden, leaped to the top of the wall and down into the field. Ah – there was the kite high in the air, its string trailing down to the ground – and there was the ball of string rolling swiftly over the grass looking exactly like a tiny animal!

Ginger raced over the field, passing poor panting Bobby on the way. The string must surely have come alive! Ginger badly wanted to pounce on it and nibble it!

The ball of string pulled along by the kite ran right across the field and over a little stream. Ginger leaped right over the water and chased the string across another field, over a stile, and down a lane. He chased it over a gate into another field – and came near to it. Near enough pounce on it and hold it!

Ah! He had got it! It seemed to wriggle beneath his paws and Ginger held on tightly. The wind pulled the kite and the kite pulled the ball of string – and Ginger felt himself being lifted half up into the air. But still he held on!

Up ran Bobby, panting hard. He fell on his knees beside Ginger and grabbed

the string too. He held it very very tightly
– and so did Ginger!

"Ginger! You caught the ball of string
for me! After I'd been horrid to you, and
shouted at you – and I was going to
smack you too! You saved my kite for
me! You're the cleverest cat in the world.
Oh dear – I'm so out-of-breath. Aren't
you?"

No – Ginger wasn't in the least out-of-breath! He rolled over on his back to be tickled. Bobby tickled him gently, and stroked him.

"You can always come and play with me and my kite now," he said. "If it hadn't been for you I'd have lost it for ever. And it's a real beauty, isn't it?"

"Miaow-ow," said Ginger, agreeing. Bobby decided to pull the kite in and go back home. So he tugged at the string and the kite came down gradually as Bobby wound in the long, long string. Soon it was flapping on the ground.

Ginger ran to it at once and put his paw on it. "Good cat! That's right. Don't let it fly any more," shouted Bobby, and Ginger felt very proud. He was sure that he knew how to fly a kite as well as Bobby!

Back they went together, Bobby, Ginger and the kite. Ginger does hope that Bobby will let him hold the string next time – but I hope he won't because I know what will happen to Ginger. He'll go flying up in the air with the kite!

# The Magic
# Sweetshop

Jo and Tom were going over Breezy Hill for a walk when they saw a narrow path going off to the west that they had never seen before.

"Hello!" said Tom, in surprise. "I've never seen that path before. Let's see where it leads, shall we, Jo?" So off they went down the funny little path. Little did they know that it was to be the beginning of a very strange adventure!

After a while they came to what looked like a tiny village – just three or four cottages set closely on the hillside with two little shops in the middle. One of them was a funny little shop with a small window of thick glass. Behind the panes were tall, thin bottles of brightly coloured sweets.

"A sweetshop," said Jo, surprised. "I didn't know there was one on this hill, did you, Tom?"

"No," said Tom. Jo pressed her nose to the window and looked at the bottles of sweets. She cried out in surprise as she read their labels.

"Tom! These are very strange sweets! Just read what they are!" Tom looked at the labels, and certainly the names of the sweets were very strange indeed. The blue sweets were labelled GIANT-SWEETS, and the pink ones DWARF-SWEETS. There were lots of other kinds too.

"You know, this must be a magic shop," said Jo, excitedly. "Let's go in and buy some! I've got a ten-pence piece and so have you."

So they pushed open the door and went inside. At first they thought there was nobody there, but then they saw a small nobbly-looking man sitting behind the counter. He had a strange tuft of hair growing straight up from his head and two long, pointed ears. His nose was long and pointed too. He was sitting by himself reading a bright-blue newspaper. "What would you like this morning?" he asked, folding up his newspaper neatly.

"Could we have ten-pence worth of mixed sweets each?" asked Tom, eagerly.

"Certainly," replied the shopman, twitching his pointed ears like a dog. He took four bottles from the window and emptied some sweets on to his scales. Jo looked at the labels on the bottles so that she would know which sweets were which. She saw him place a giant-sweet, a dwarf-sweet, an invisible-sweet, and a home-again-sweet into the scales.

The children felt very excited when the shopman handed each of them a bag. He took their money and put it into a tin box. Then he picked up his blue newspaper and began to read again.

"What will happen to us if we eat these sweets?" Tom asked the little man, but all he would say was, "Try, and see!"

The children didn't like to ask him anything else so they went outside and walked up the little crooked street. They were surprised when they came to a big white gate that went right across the road.

"This is stranger and stranger," said Tom. "I've never seen that village before, and now here is a gate that I've never seen before either."

"Shall we climb over?" said Jo. "We are nearly at the top of the hill."

"Yes, let's," said Tom. To their great surprise, they saw a town on the other side!

"How strange!" said Jo. "There has never been anything on the other side of this hill before!"

They went on down towards the town, and soon met some most peculiar-looking people. They were very round, and their arms were very long indeed. Their faces were as red as tomatoes and they wore big white ruffs round their necks, which made their faces seem redder than ever.

Some of them were riding in small motor-cars, rather like toy ones but with sunshades instead of proper hoods. Jo and Tom stood in the middle of the road and stared in astonishment.

A motor-car with a bright-yellow hood came along at a tremendous pace. Tom jumped to one side, but Jo was just too late and the little car ran right into her. To her great amazement it exploded in to a hundred pieces!

The little round man in the car shot up in the air and down again. He landed on the ground with a bump and he *was* cross!

"You silly, stupid, foolish, ridiculous girl!" he cried. "Why didn't you get out of my way? Look what you've done to my car? It's gone pop!"

"Well," said Jo, getting up. "I'm sorry, but you were driving too fast. You didn't even hoot."

"You horrid, nasty, rude, selfish girl!" cried the little man, getting even crosser.

"Hey!" said Tom. "Don't speak to Jo like that! Haven't you any manners? You might have hurt her very much running into her like that!"

The little round man went quite purple with rage. He took a trumpet from his pocket and blew loudly on it. *Tan-tara! Tan-tara!*

At once a whole crowd of funny-looking people came running up and took hold of Jo and Tom.

"Take them to prison!" shouted the man whose motor-car had exploded.

"Give them nothing but bread and water for sixty days!"

The children could do nothing against so many, so they were marched off to a big yellow building, and locked up in a tiny cell. Tom banged on the door but it was no use. It was locked and bolted on the outside.

"Look here, Jo!" said Tom, suddenly. "Let's eat one of these sweets each. Perhaps something will happen to help us!"

So they each picked a blue sweet from their bags and put it into their mouths.

And before long a very curious thing happened! They began to grow taller. Yes, and fatter, too! In fact their heads soon touched the ceiling.

"I say! Those must have been the sweets out of the giant-sweet bottle!" said Tom, in excitement.

He kicked at the door and it almost broke, for his feet were now very big.

"Stop that!" cried an angry voice outside. "If you kick your door again, prisoners, I shall not give you any supper!"

"Ho!" said Tom, pleased. "I shall certainly kick it again! Then when it's opened, Jo, we'll walk out and give everyone a shock!"

*Bang, bang, bang!* He kicked the door hard again. At once it was unbolted and unlocked and a very angry keeper came in. But when he saw how big the children were, his red face turned quite pale and he ran away as fast as his little legs would carry him!

Tom and Jo squeezed out of the door and went down the street. How they

laughed to see the astonishment on the faces of the townsfolk, who now looked very small indeed.

Soon they came to a crossroads. There was a signpost, and on it was printed: TO GIANTLAND.

"Goodness!" said Jo. "How exciting! We are giants now, Tom. Do let's take this road and see if we can find some other giants."

So the children set off, feeling more and more excited. After half an hour they came to some enormous trees and realised that they must have arrived in Giantland.

Soon after that they saw a giant – but

dear me, the giants were far bigger than the children had guessed they would be! In fact, they were enormous! They towered over the children.

A very large giant with eyes like dinner plates saw them first. He gaped at Tom and Jo in surprise and then called to his friends nearby in a voice like thunder:

"HEY! LOOK HERE! HERE ARE SOME STRANGE CHILDREN!"

Immediately the children were surrounded by a dozen huge giants. They didn't like it at all. One of the giants poked his finger into Tom's chest.

"HE'S REAL," he said, in a booming voice. "HE'S NOT A DOLL."

"Of course I'm not a doll!" shouted Tom, crossly. "Don't poke me like that!"

It amused the giants to see how cross Tom was, and they poked him again and again with their big, bony fingers.

"Aren't they nasty, unkind creatures," cried Jo, for she didn't like the great giants with their enormous eyes and teeth like piano keys. "Oh, Tom, can't we escape?"

"How can we?" said Tom, trying to push away a finger that came to tickle him. "Oh, I know, Jo! Let's eat another sweet!"

In a great hurry the children took out their sweet bags and ate a pink sweet each. In an instant they felt themselves growing smaller and smaller – smaller and smaller. The giants seemed to grow bigger and bigger and bigger. Soon they were so big that they seemed like mountains! The children were tinier than sparrows to the giants – tinier than ladybirds even!

"Quick!" said Jo, catching hold of Tom's hand. "Let's go somewhere safe before they tread on us!"

There was a large hole in the ground not far from them and Jo and Tom ran to it. It seemed like a dark tunnel to them,

but really it was only a wormhole!

Down the tunnel they went, meeting huge worms and other giant creatures as they went. A great beetle hurried by them, treading heavily on Jo's toes. It was all rather alarming.

"I wish we could get out of here," said Tom, after a time. "Oh look, Jo! There's a tiny pinhole of light far ahead of us. That must be where the wormhole ends. Come on!"

On they went and at last came out into the sunshine on a green hillside, and nearby was a notice saying:

BROOMSTICK HILL
ALL TRESPASSERS WILL BE
TURNED INTO SNAILS

"Ooh!" said Jo in alarm. "Look at that!"

But they hardly had time to read the notice before there was a strange whirring noise up above them. To the children's enormous surprise about a hundred witches came flying through the sky on broomsticks. They darkened the sky like a black cloud.

The witches were heading for the green hillside and, of course, the very first thing their sharp eyes saw was Jo, with her golden-yellow hair. Tom had hidden quickly behind a bush, but Jo was so surprised to see the witches that she hadn't even thought of hiding!

As the witches came rushing over towards them, Tom pulled Jo down beside him.

"Get out your sweet bag and eat a sweet!" he whispered. "We've got two left. Eat the purple one and we'll see what happens!"

"Where is that trespassing child!" cried the witches. "We will turn her into a snail! How dare she come to our hillside!"

Jo and Tom popped the purple sweets into their mouths. They looked around – and to their surprise they couldn't see each other. At first they didn't know what had happened, and then they guessed – the sweets had made them invisible!

The children ran off down the hill. When they looked back at the witches, they were hunting in astonishment all around the bush where they had seen Jo.

"There's no one here!" they cried. "Where has she gone?"

By this time Jo and Tom were at the bottom of the hill. As they could not see one another, they held each others hands very firmly.

"I'm tired of this adventure," said Jo, at last. "We always seem to be chased by

159

something – funny people, or giants, or witches. Goodness knows what it will be next time! Can't we go home now, Tom?"

"But we don't know the way," said Tom, looking around. "I'm hungry and I'd love to go home. I wish I did know the way! However are we going to get home again, Jo?"

"I know," said Jo, feeling for her sweet bag. "Let's eat the last sweet, shall we, Tom, and see what happens."

So the children put their last sweet – a red one – into their mouths and before they had finished eating it they could see one another again! They were so pleased, for they were both tired of being invisible!

Tom and Jo waited patiently to see what else would happen. Would a big wind come and carry them home? Or perhaps a fairy carriage pulled by butterflies would arrive to help them. They waited and waited, but nothing happened. They looked at each other and sighed.

Jo and Tom just went on sitting there

at the bottom of the hill, waiting in the
sunshine. But still nothing happened. It
was very strange.

Perhaps the home-again-sweets
wouldn't take them home after all? If
not, how would they get there? They
were quite sure they would never be able
to find the way by themselves!

Then Jo began to look around her. She
saw a big fir tree that she seemed to
know. She noticed a house not far off
that looked familiar, and she was sure

she recognised the pathway leading up the hill. Suddenly she jumped up with a cry of delight.

"Tom! We are home! This is the hill just outside our own garden! That's our house over there! Why, we've been home all the time and didn't know it! However could we have got here? I'm sure the hill outside our garden isn't really a witch's hill."

They were astonished, but it was quite true – they really were home again. They were just outside their own garden. They could see their mother standing at the front door.

"Well, how surprising!" said Tom, standing up and brushing himself down. "We're safely back after our adventures. Let's go and tell Mum. Perhaps she'll come with us this evening and see that funny sweetshop on the hillside."

The children ran home and told their mother all about their strange adventures. That evening they all went up the hillside to find the sweetshop. They followed the little path – but alas, it did not lead to a sweetshop at all; only to a great many rabbit-holes!

"It's just a rabbit path!" said Mother. "You must have dreamed it all, my dears!"

But they didn't really, you know!

# Teddy
# and the Elves

There was a new radio in the playroom. It had only just arrived, and the children were very excited about it. They had never had a radio before.

"You just press this button here to turn it on," Emma explained to her little brother John. She pressed the round red button on the front. There was a little click and, to the astonishment of the toys who were listening, a band started to play. Teddy stared at the radio in surprise. The rag-doll almost fell off the shelf, and the yellow cat was so frightened by the noise that she hid behind the blue dog.

The children were delighted with their radio. It had been given to them the day before by their Uncle John.

164

"May Emma and I keep it on, Mummy?" asked John.

"Yes – but not too loudly," said his mother. "And make sure you keep it somewhere safe," she added. "I had a nice little radio that I kept on the shelf in the kitchen and it has completely disappeared. So has my best blue and white egg cup, and some of my silver spoons. You haven't seen them, have you children? I can't think where they can have gone."

But the children weren't listening to their mother. They were busy twiddling the knob on the front of the radio, instead, to see what different music they could find.

The toys thought the radio was wonderful. They listened to it all that day and all the next, and so did the children. They heard all sorts of different music and sometimes people even spoke out of the radio. The toys simply could not understand how they got in there. At other times, someone played the piano, and that seemed amazing too. How could a piano get inside such a small thing?

At night, when the children had gone to bed, the teddy bear looked longingly at the radio.

"It's magic," he said to the others. "It must be magic. How else can it have all those people inside it? I wish I could open it up and see exactly what is in there. How do you suppose you open it, Rag-Doll?"

"Don't even think of such a thing!"

166

cried the rag-doll in horror. "You might break it."

"No, I won't," said Teddy, and he began to undo a screw at the back. The rag-doll had to get the big sailor doll to come and help stop him.

"We shall put you inside the brick-box, if you don't solemnly promise to leave the radio alone from now on," said the rag-doll. Teddy didn't want to be put into the brick-box, so he had to promise.

But the next night Teddy wanted to press the red button that made the radio play. "I want to see the light come on,

and hear the music play," he said. "Please let me press the button!"

"What! And wake up everyone in the house and have them rushing in here to see what's going on?" cried the rag-doll. "You must be mad."

"But they wouldn't hear it," said the teddy bear. "Oh, do let me try. I promise to keep it quiet."

"You really are a very, very naughty teddy," said the rag-doll. "You are not to press that button at all."

For the next two nights the teddy bear was quite good. But on the following night, he waited until the toys were playing quietly in the other corner of the room, then he crept over to the radio and pressed the button. The light shone inside and loud music began to play!

The toys were horrified! Clockwork Clown and Sailor Doll rushed over at once and pressed the button again. The light went out and the music stopped.

"Teddy! How naughty of you!" cried the sailor doll. "If you're not careful you will wake up the whole family. If they

catch us, we will never be able to come to life at night again!"

But Teddy didn't care. "They wouldn't have heard it," he said. "It is you with your big shouting voice that will wake everyone up!" And he ran off into the corner, squeezed himself under the children's piano, and refused to come out.

After that, Teddy wouldn't speak to any of the others, not even the little clockwork mouse who loved to chatter to him. It was very sad. Soon nobody asked him to join in the games, and the teddy bear began to feel very lonely indeed.

Deep down, Teddy knew that he should apologise to the sailor doll, and to all the other toys. But he was a proud teddy bear and he could not bring himself to say sorry.

Then one night, when the moon shone brightly outside the playroom window, Teddy could stand it no longer. He tried to join in with a game that the toys were playing, but they just ignored him.

Teddy was very upset. He walked away. "Very well!" he called over his shoulder. "If you won't play with me I'm going to find somewhere else to live!"

Out of the playroom door he went. The toys stared after him in horror. No toy ever went out of the playroom at night. Whatever was Teddy thinking of?

The moon shone brightly, and the

teddy bear could see quite plainly where he was going. He went down the stairs, jumping them one at a time. They seemed very steep! He reached the bottom and looked round. Emma had sometimes taken him downstairs. He knew there was a room called the kitchen that had a nice smell in it. Which way was it?

Teddy found the kitchen door and squeezed round it. He was just about to cross the room when a shadow fell across the moonlit floor.

Teddy looked up in surprise. Had the moon gone behind a cloud?

No, it hadn't. It was somebody on the windowsill, blocking out the moon – and that somebody was climbing in the kitchen window! The teddy bear stared in surprise. Who could it be, coming in through the kitchen window in the middle of the night?

"It must be a robber!" thought Teddy in dismay. "They come in the night sometimes, and steal things. Oh dear, whatever shall I do? The toys will be even more cross with me if I make a noise and wake everyone up. Oh dear, oh dear, oh dear!"

Meanwhile, do you know who it was climbing in through the window? Why, it was three naughty little elves. They sprang quietly to the floor, and were busy trying to open the larder door.

Usually, they only came to the kitchen looking for bits of food – a slice of currant cake, perhaps, or some biscuits. But sometimes, when they were feeling very naughty, they took other things too. Only the week before they had taken some things from one of the kitchen shelves and hidden them in the garden, but tonight they had only come to look for things to eat. Teddy watched as they started to fill their little knapsacks with food – sticky buns, pieces of cheese, and even some of Emma's favourite sweets.

Then one of the elves jumped up onto a shelf and started to pick up all sorts of other things for his knapsack – paper clips, a little key, a coloured crayon. Then he held something up that sparkled in the moonlight.

"Hello!" he said. "Look what I've found!" Teddy was dismayed to see that the elf was holding a beautiful ring which he quickly put into his knapsack.

"It must belong to Emma's mother," thought Teddy to himself. "She will be so sad to lose it."

And right there and then he decided that something must be done, so while the elves were still busy filling their knapsacks. Teddy slipped out of the kitchen and hurried upstairs as fast as he could go.

When he reached the playroom, he rushed through the door, panting. The toys looked at him in amazement.

"What's the matter? You look quite pale!" said the panda.

"Quick! Quick! There are three elves downstairs taking things from the kitchen!" cried the teddy. "We must stop them. Let's wake the humans up! Come on, make a noise everyone!"

All at once the toys started shouting.

The panda growled as loudly as he could. The jack-in-the-box jumped up and down and banged his box on the floor. The toy mouse squeaked. But it was no good. No one could hear them.

No one woke up. Not a sound could be heard.

And then Teddy did a most peculiar thing! He gave a little cry, and rushed over to the radio. Before the toys could stop him, he pressed the little red button – and then he turned one of the knobs right round as far as it would go! The light went on inside the radio and a tremendous noise came blaring out!

It was a man's voice, giving the midnight news; but the teddy bear had put the radio on so loudly that it was as if the man was shouting at the top of his voice.

"This will wake them up!" said Teddy.

And so it did! It also frightened the elves in the kitchen so much that they dropped the contents of their knapsacks all over the floor and made a terrible noise trying to scramble out of the window.

But by the time Emma's father had got to the kitchen, they had quite gone.

"Must be those mice again!" sighed Emma's father, staring at the mess on the floor. Then something shiny caught his eye and he was surprised to find a ring lying among the crumbs.

Upstairs in the playroom, Emma and John were turning off the radio.

"This is what woke us up, Daddy," said John when his father appeared. "The playroom radio. But who could have put it on?"

Nobody knew. But Emma caught a gleam in Teddy's eye as he sat by the toy-cupboard. Could he possibly have turned on the radio? Emma knew quite well she had put him back into the toy cupboard that evening – and there he was, sitting outside it! If she hadn't been old enough to know that toys can't walk and talk, she would have felt sure he had been up to something!

"The elves have gone. They won't come back after that fright!" cried the toys once everyone had gone back to bed.

"Good old Teddy! What a noise the radio made, didn't it?"

Teddy was delighted to find himself such a hero. He beamed all over his face.

"Perhaps we can all be friends again now," he said hopefully.

"Oh, yes let's!" cried all the toys together. "It's so much nicer."

"And perhaps every so often you'll let me turn the radio on at night ever so quietly," added Teddy, smiling.

"All right," said the sailor doll. "You deserve a reward, Teddy. You really were very clever."

Everyone agreed. And now when he feels like listening to a little music, the teddy bear turns the radio knob – very gently – and the music comes whispering out. Emma and John will be surprised if they hear it, won't they?

# Wanted – A Royal
# Snow-digger

Once upon a time the Fairy Queen wanted
a Royal Snow-digger, who would dig away
the snow from her palace gates after a
snowstorm. So she sent out Domino the
brownie and told him to find somebody.
Off he went, the feather in his cap waving
merrily. He was sure that anyone would be
pleased to be made Royal Snow-digger to
Her Majesty the Queen.

First he went to Slicker the grass
snake, who lay basking in the sunshine of
the pretty autumn day.

"Slicker," he said, "will you be Royal
Snow-digger to the Queen, and dig away
the snow from the palace gates after a
snowstorm?"

"What is snow?" asked Slicker in
wonder. "I have never seen it. I sleep all

179

the winter through, Domino, in the hollow tree over there, curled up with my brothers and sisters. I cannot be Royal Snow-digger."

Domino ran off, disappointed. He went to the cornfield where Dozy the little dormouse used to live – but Dozy had run from the field when the corn was cut and was now in the hazel copse, hunting for fallen nuts. Domino found him there, as fat as butter.

"Dozy," he said, "will you be Royal Snow-digger to the Queen and dig away the snow from the palace gates after a snowstorm?"

"Not I!" said Dozy, rubbing his fat little sides. "I shall sleep all the winter through. See how fat I am! I shall not need any food all the cold-weather time. It is stupid to wake up when it is cold. Far better to sleep. I shall be hidden in a warm bank down in a cosy hole, Domino, when the snow comes. I don't want to dig snow for the Queen."

Domino ran off, quite cross with the fat little dormouse. He came to where the

swallows flew high in the air, and called
to them, for he knew that the Fairy
Queen was fond of the steel-blue birds.

"Swallows," he called, "will you be
Royal Snow-digger to the Queen and dig
away the snow from the palace gates
after a snowstorm?"

"Twitter, twitter, Domino!" called the
swallows, laughing. "Why, we shall not be
here much longer! We never wait for

snow and frost. It is too cold for us in the wintertime here, and besides there are no flies to eat. No, no, we are going to fly away south, far away to the warm countries where nobody has ever seen such a strange thing as snow."

Domino sighed. He would never find a snow-digger for the Queen. It was strange. He wondered who to ask next.

"I'll ask the big badger," he thought. "He would make a fine snow-digger, for he has great paws, strong and sturdy."

So he went to where the badger was walking on the hillside and called to him.

"Hey, Brock the badger!" he cried. "Will you be Royal Snow-digger to the

Queen and dig away the snow from the palace gates after a snowstorm?"

"I should like to very much," said Brock. "But, you know, Domino, I cannot keep awake in the wintertime. I simply have to go to sleep. I am lining a nice big hole in the hillside now, with all sorts of warm things – dead leaves and bracken and big cushions of moss – to make me and my family a warm bed for the winter. We always sleep through the cold weather."

"Dear, dear, what lazy creatures you must be!" said Domino, crossly. "Well, I'll go and find someone else. They can't all be as lazy as you, Brock!"

Soon Domino met the hedgehog, Spiny, and he waved his hand to him brightly.

"Hey, Spiny!" he called. "Wait a minute! I want to ask you something. Will you be Royal Snow-digger to the Queen and dig away the snow from the palace gates after a snowstorm?"

"I'd like to, Domino," said Spiny, shuffling in the dead leaves. "But you know, I hide away in the ditch all winter

183

through. I can't bear the cold weather. You won't find me after a snowstorm! No, I cannot be Royal Snow-digger. But look – there goes Crawler the toad. Ask him."

The toad was crawling on the damp side of the ditch, so Domino jumped across and spoke to him.

"Crawler, will you be Royal Snow-digger to the Queen and dig away the snow from the palace gates after a snowstorm?" he asked.

"No," said Crawler, blinking his lovely coppery eyes, "I won't. I am a sensible person and I like to sleep under a damp stone when frost and snow are about. It's no use asking my cousins the frogs, either – they sleep upside-down in the pond, tucked comfortably away in the mud at the bottom. Goodbye!"

"There aren't many more people to ask," said Domino to himself. "Dear, dear me – I can't possibly go home to the Queen and tell her that I can find nobody. She would make me Royal Snow-digger and that's a job I should hate! Too much

hard work about it for me! Hello, there goes Bushy the squirrel. He's a lively chap. He'd make a splendid snow-digger."

So he called to Bushy the squirrel, who was hiding nuts away in a hollow tree.

"Bushy! Bushy! Will you be Royal

Snow-digger and sweep away the snow from the palace gate after a snowstorm?" he called. "You don't sleep all the winter, do you?"

"Well, not exactly," said the squirrel. "But I only wake up on nice sunny days, Domino. I sleep curled up in my tail in a hollow tree when it's really cold. I'm not sure I would wake up after a snowstorm. In fact, I'm quite sure I couldn't. But you can try to wake me if you like."

"Oh no, thanks," said Domino, in disgust. "I must have someone I can trust to be on the spot. I don't want to go hunting in all the hollow trees in the wood to find you on a snowy day!"

He turned away and went back towards the palace. As he went he heard a little voice calling him. He looked round. It was Bobtail the sandy rabbit.

"I heard what you were asking Bushy the squirrel," said Bobtail. "Do you think I would do for Royal Snow-digger, Domino? I'd love to try."

"Oh, I expect you sleep all the winter, don't you, like the others?" said Domino, gloomily. "Or you stand on your head in the pond? Or line a hole in a bank and snore there? I don't believe there's any use in asking you to be Royal Snow-digger."

"Oh, Domino, I keep awake all the winter!" said Bobtail. "Yes, I do, really.

I'm used to the snow. And there is my cousin the hare, too – he's out all the winter. And so are the weasels and the stoats – but don't let's talk of them! They are cruel fellows, and no gentlemen!"

"Well, you can be Royal Snow-digger then," said Domino. "Come along to the Queen and she will give you your snow-digger badge. But mind, Bobtail, if you suddenly make up your mind to do what nearly all the others do – sleep, or fly away, or hide somewhere – I'll hunt you out and pull your tail."

"I shan't do any of those things," said Bobtail, happily. He walked to the palace with Domino the brownie, and the Queen hung a little golden badge round his neck: on it was printed ROYAL SNOW-DIGGER.

And now every winter the rabbits are the Queen's snow-diggers. They sweep away the snow from the palace gates after a snowstorm, and never dream of going to sleep like the toads and hedgehogs, the badgers and the squirrels.

If you see a rabbit out in the snow, look at him carefully. If he has a golden badge hung round his neck, you'll know what he is – a Royal Snow-digger!